Herod's Wife

A Deep South Book

Other books by Madison Jones

The Innocent
Forest of the Night
A Buried Land
An Exile
A Cry of Absence
Passage through Gehenna
Season of the Strangler
Last Things
To the Winds
Nashville 1864: The Dying of the Light

Herod's Wife
A Novel

Madison Jones

Madison Jones (signature)

THE UNIVERSITY OF ALABAMA PRESS
Tuscaloosa and London

Copyright © 2003
The University of Alabama Press
Tuscaloosa, Alabama 35487-0380
All rights reserved
Manufactured in the United States of America

Typeface: AJenson

∞

The paper on which this book is printed meets the minimum
requirements of American National Standard for Information
Science-Permanence of Paper for Printed Library Materials, ANSI
Z39.48-1984.

Library of Congress Cataloging-in-Publication Data

Jones, Madison, 1925–
Herod's wife : a novel / Madison Jones.
p. cm. — (Deep South books)
ISBN 0-8173-1298-6 (alk. paper)
ISBN 0-8173-5014-4 (pbk. : alk. paper)
1. Southern States—Fiction. I. Title. II. Series.

PS3560.O517 H47 2003
813'.54—dc21   002155284

British Library Cataloguing-in-Publication Data available

For my beloved wife Shailah,
whose unfailing help has made many things possible.

Herod's Wife

I

The two of them, Hugh and Nora Helton, both nude and half-covered by the bedsheet, had been lying there open-eyed and silent for quite some time now. It was not a new thing that, despite his urgent desire, their intercourse had been less than satisfactory. The fact was as plain as if it had been spelled out where their common gaze was fastened, on a ceiling tinted a pallid rose by evening light filtered through the curtains. Hugh was waiting. He knew that at any moment she would speak and he would hear the words, the familiar words, delivered in the husky voice that would grow more passionate as she spoke. Finally it came.

"You have got to get over it, Hugh. It's coming between us. Seriously. It's crippling to us."

A new word there, "crippling." An apt one, though.

She was looking at him now, her dark eyes brightening with vexation. "Can't you get it through your head that nobody cares anymore? Except some bumpkin Baptists and that obsolete church of yours. Your nosy little priest. Who is he to condemn you? I'll bet he has a girlfriend somewhere. Or a boyfriend."

"Probably not," Hugh barely murmured.

She ignored this. Turning onto her side to face him now, she said, "Look at our friends. Half of them divorced or about to be. And why not, if they don't get along? What kind of benighted notion is it that two people should go on living together all their lives in misery? Not me. I had come to really despise Wilbur. A long time before we moved here and I met you."

Now, with her eyes more acutely trained on his face, she stopped. She was reading him . . . reading him accurately, he knew. "All right," she said, releasing a breath. "Here we are again, back in the Old Testament." Then, sarcastically, "Married to your brother's wife. Incest, isn't it? Alas . . . It was all right, though, when you were humping me before we married."

"Not quite all right," he murmured. "I guess maybe I thought those feelings would go away if we got married."

A little grimace stretched the corners of her mouth. "So that's why you married me. So we could go right on and you not feel guilty."

"No," he said with more energy now. "That's not true. I married you because I love you. You were different. In my forty-two years I never had met a woman who really moved me . . . not like you. Different . . . and so beautiful." And this was true, every way. The bedsheet had slipped farther down, exposing the graceful torso, slightly arched, and flesh that in this filtered light made him think of mother-of-pearl.

His words had touched her, softened the gaze fixed on him. Not for long, though. Her voice had the same edge to it. "But I haven't changed your old feelings, have I? They keep right on." A moment later, with her eyes still on him, she settled onto the pillow and lay in silence.

Hugh was silent too, gazing up at the ceiling. Silence was all he heard, inside and outside the house. No distant church bell ringing, though, he thought, it must be close to five o'clock and the Sunday evening Mass. He had stopped attending at all some months ago, and even before that, for a long time, he had refused communion. Excommunicated. A big word that once upon a time had held real meaning for him. He envisioned the small church building, isolated among maple trees, and old Father Connerly stuttering his way through the Mass. Even then it was a church struggling to stay alive in a community that was overwhelmingly Protestant. A struggle still harder now, when indifference to religion, it seemed, held sway everywhere. Poor young Father Riley, in more than one way an alien in these parts. In his first year or so, he and Hugh had been friends, of a sort. Until the break, that unpleasant day, the intrusion into Hugh's life that had not only shattered the friendship but left him with a residue of resentment amounting sometimes to bitterness.

Hugh suddenly recalled that there was a question hanging. He had just got a grip on what it was when Nora's voice, by its sharpness first, surprised him.

"Maybe the time has come when you should choose between me and your feelings."

It took him a moment, parsing his answer. "That's nonsense. I choose you. And I always will." After a stillness, "It'll pass off. It just comes by spells, now; it's not near like it was at first. Reason finally takes hold."

"Well, hurry it up," she said. "And tell that damned priest to stop sending you those stupid tracts. Do you read them?"

"I just glanced at them. There haven't been but two."

"There was one yesterday. I got through the first paragraph before I threw it in the trash." She drew a breath and, as though between clenched teeth, said, "The nerve of that little bastard . . . trying to break up our marriage. Could he have been taught to do such things? That church should be exterminated." The flush of anger was suddenly vivid in her neck and cheeks. "I'll bet he bad-mouths us every chance he gets."

"Don't worry," Hugh calmly said. "Who would listen to him, anyway? It's not like he was 'somebody' in this town."

With an emphasis even harsher Nora said, "I wish him in *hell*."

"Let's forget about him," Hugh mumbled and got out of bed and went into the bathroom.

The view from these west windows upstairs included not only the whole central part of town but a good portion of the lake beyond. In part it was this view that had made him hasten, once the way to their marriage was clear, to buy and renovate this handsome old house halfway up a long and partly wooded hill-slope where, so far, only a few scattered houses stood. Even after several months of living here, and especially in the privacy of the bathroom, he would find himself arrested in contemplation of the panorama spread out below him. These were intervals in which he would often experience a curious shift or confusion of moods, responses. Even in this bright summer weather there were times when across a mood of contentment shadows would drift and darken the prospect in his eyes. In such poignant moments he would envision the village of his youth and a river still a river not yet swollen into a lake. Like a flood, he would think, that overnight engulfed the town and, receding, left in its place a small metropolis of unfamiliar eager faces intent on business or merriment, of sleek store fronts and neon lights and marinas humming with the sound of motors all along the lakefront. Like a miracle, like a wizard's work, performed in the blink of an eye.

And so . . . ? he would say to himself, spurning these moments of regret. For what had with such violence seized and transformed that village was life as it really was, had come to be, and regret was futile dreaming. No doubt had this life not come to him of itself, he, and the likes of him, would have left this place to find it. But it had come and he had reaped the fruits: success beyond expectation in his law practice, new friends more to his taste, this elegant old house, and crowning it all, this woman like no other.

An approaching car that slowed as it drew near got his attention. It stopped in front of the gate and Jean, Nora Jean, got out, then paused for a word or two with the invisible driver. He watched her, thinking as he so often did that here was the nearest thing to trouble on his horizon these days. He had tried and tried to make friends, but without any luck so far; his mere approach was like a signal warning her to fall silent. He comforted himself with the thought that, considering her devotion to her mother, it was not unnatural, was something time would resolve. Maybe. For it did not bode well that, by report, her actual father had fared little better than he. So he thought, watching her progress up the walk, noting how like her mother she was in both looks and grace of movement.

Hugh stepped from the bathroom to the sight of Nora, fresh out of bed and still naked, standing motionless in quarter-profile to him. An image from his scant knowledge of mythology came to mind: it was Venus risen from the sea, all aglow with the filtered sunset light. But her voice (she too had been observing the scene down there) cut short his moment of resurging desire. "Jean just now got out of somebody's car down there. Did you happen to notice?"

"Yes, by chance."

"Could you tell if the driver was an older man, Mr. Needham . . . her ballet teacher?"

"No. I couldn't see him."

"I don't remember his having a car like that. He's always been the one to drive her home from her lessons. I don't like those boys who keep trying to date her."

"She's old enough to take care of herself," Hugh said.

"I don't trust them."

"She'll be careful. For your sake, if nothing else. Not many mothers have the hold on their daughters that you've got." Then, "Get dressed and let's go down for a drink. Maybe Jean will agree to sit with us, for a change."

2

Father John Riley was a lonely young man, especially since his appointment here in Lakepoint more than two years ago. This was not a state of mind entirely new to him, however. There had not been many Catholics in his own hometown six hundred miles north of here, in Michigan, and from his early teens when he received the first hints of what he soon identified as a calling, he had felt himself in some measure set apart. In his days at a state college this feeling only intensified, and immediately after graduation he enrolled in the Catholic Seminary in Lansing. Those were his happiest days, when he could share his thoughts and feelings with fellow seminarians and form real and lasting friendships.

After ordination, Father Riley's first assignment, lasting nearly two years, was to a parish there in Lansing, as assistant pastor. The older priest was a pious and dedicated man, and his young assistant, receptive as he was, learned to follow close in his footsteps. Two other assignments, one in St. Louis and one in Memphis, occupied the years until he was thirty and was transferred to this tiny parish here in Lakepoint. Why, when he was young and energetic and much better fit for a larger parish? He smothered his vexation, remembering the stress and confusion under which the church had to operate in these pagan times.

At least, however, he had come here with the expectation of finding, in this relatively small southern town, a community still more or less intact. He quickly saw that his expectation was groundless. Of the fifteen or so families that made up his congregation, no more than half were staunch Catholics in the sense that he had hoped for. By and large they were impatient with ritual, half-ignorant of church doctrine, and all but openly in rebellion against the teachings on such matters as divorce and birth control. Witness to this last was how few children they had. And in fact it was the children themselves, or most of them, who best represented the spiritual failings of their parents. This was something Father Riley discovered early on, as soon as he established weekly classes for their instruction. Even in these classes discipline was hard to enforce. But it was not this, or even their ignorance, that truly alarmed him. It was a deeper thing, something he sensed: a certain coarse grain of cynicism dismaying in the young.

Such were Father Riley's burdens. He dealt with them, directly or otherwise, as best he could in his homilies, observing from his pulpit the faces of his scattered congregation. He saw interest here and there but also indifference, and sometimes, at mention of certain topics, barely veiled expressions of hostility or skepticism. Although it had happened elsewhere in the past, somehow he was especially surprised when his first mention of Satan, that evil being at war with God and man, was one of these. But even in his most uncomfortable moments in the pulpit there was one thing that always inspired him. It was the beauty of this small chapel, the sift of light through the stained and embossed windows, the handsome image of the Virgin standing serene in her little grotto, the Stations of the Cross carved in what seemed to be the purest ivory. Those responsible for all this must surely have loved the Lord.

He managed to keep busy most of the time. In addition to his strict priestly duties, he visited his congregation in their homes and on occasion in the small hospital, where he also offered his services to any and all. Besides his private quarters out back, with a little help from old Mrs. Galleger he cleaned the church building daily. He tended the small graveyard beside the church and also plots of grass and shrubbery in unshaded spaces between the maple trees. The trees were large, for maples, casting wide areas of dense shade. He took much pleasure in these trees, thinking of them as one more expression of the love that had built this chapel. And there were his almost daily walks, out into the country or maybe through town where he sometimes stopped for a meal at the Lakeview Restaurant.

These things, along with some reading, almost filled his days, but more and more he wished for a real friend or two. For quite a while he had believed that he almost had one. Until a coolness, unexplained at first, set in between them. Hugh Helton, an old communicant, following in the steps of his parents before him. He had ceased all of a sudden to take communion. Then the long interval in which even his presence at Mass was erratic, and at last his permanent absence. For a time Father Riley had tried, but there was no approaching him anymore. He wondered in vain until the day when the gossip reached him. A little inquiry confirmed the truth of it, the shocking truth.

It was not merely that Hugh was to marry a divorced woman; this was a sin now regarded as practically routine. More shocking for Father Riley was the fact that the woman was Hugh's brother's wife, snatched, as it were, from his brother's arms. Pondering his revulsion at the news, Father Riley searched his memory for teachings that might apply to the case. He found nothing, nothing except the strictures of Old Testament law. But his revulsion persisted, like the ghost of an odor that he was unable quite to expel from his nostrils. In any case, and substantive enough, the sin of betrayal was there, of violence against a brother. After some days of near obsession with the matter Father Riley had come to a decision. But another whole day of uncertainty passed before he had set out to execute it. This was many months ago but every detail of it, seemingly, remained fast in his mind.

Around four o'clock in the afternoon he stopped in front of a building, one in a row of nearly new brickfronts, that had Attorney-at-Law written on the door glass. Foolish and futile, he thought, brazen like nothing he had ever done before. He clenched his teeth and went in.

From behind a desk where a nameplate said Ms. Renaldo, a bright face enclosed in frosted curls looked up at him, then registered faint surprise. It was his clerical garb; he had thought this best for the occasion. He declared himself and watched her rise and, with a courteous smile, turn and pass through a door behind her.

She was a long time about it. He heard voices through the door. This meant refusal, flat rejection, he thought, and felt a moment of release. She appeared, stood looking at him with a sort of puzzled courtesy. "He'll see you now, sir."

Hugh did not get up from behind his large and cluttered desk. His posture in the swivel chair conveyed an ambiguous impression, something between relaxed and guardedly alert. "Father John," he finally said, just as if to identify this man. Then, in nearly an undertone, "Sit down."

Father Riley did so, in a cushioned chair close by, hearing the door fall shut behind him. How to start? He saw that Hugh was determined not to be the first to speak. Father Riley said, hearing the fatuous words come off his tongue, "You're looking well."

"I'm well enough."

Indeed he did look so: his face and what was visible of his rangy body were not so gaunt as in the past, and even his reddish hair appeared to have lost its patches of gray. Finally, "I hope you'll forgive me for intruding this way . . . into personal things. It's just that we were friends . . . and I feel so strongly . . ."

". . . that I need a lecture," Hugh finished, in a perfectly flat voice.

It was not unexpected, this hostility, but he had no words prepared. He said, "We were friends, you know, and I hoped that I . . ."

". . . could persuade me," Hugh said, just as before. "And keep me from going to hell."

"I wouldn't put it that way, Hugh."

"It's what you mean." Hugh stirred and rested a hand on the edge of the desk. There was a thin gold band on his ring finger. Engagement? Close by, one elegant red rose stood in a narrow vase.

"That is a teaching of the church," Father Riley quietly said, "but there's more I wish you'd think about . . . at least to . . ." He faltered for a moment. Behind him through the shut door he could just hear the secretary's voice, talking to someone, interrupted by a small burst of laughter. More firmly he said, "It's that I can't believe you'll be able to find happiness, contentment, this way. You've been a Christian, a good Catholic all your life. And your people before you. I always felt I knew you well . . . I still do. And that your faith had deep roots, deeper than you may think." He faltered again, conscious of the eyes, brown and steady, fastened on him.

"It's not only your marrying a divorced woman, Hugh. There's your brother to think about. To me that's almost worse, because he's your brother . . . that you took her away from." He added, "And more, too. The example you set. Evil like this, all evil, is infectious. You know that. This society, so-called, is a moral chaos already."

Hugh listened without a blink, waiting, waiting for him to finish. After a silence he took his hand off the desk and sat a little straighter. "Father John, let's get it over with. I've quit the church for good . . . and its teachings, most of them. I didn't do it without thinking. I don't believe in miracles and haven't for a while. I think the church is done for . . . irrelevant, obsolete. Reasonable people see this and make their own values. We're making our own world now." He paused. "Look at the misery you cause, things we could get rid of easy. Like about divorce and remarriage. Why should Nora (that's her name) have gone on in a marriage that was miserable and getting worse. And why shouldn't I marry her? And by the way, I didn't 'take' her away from him." In this pause he blinked for what seemed the first time. "As for my brother, Wilbur, he had it coming, the way he treated her. If he hates me, it's his fault."

In the silence Father Riley sat there gazing not at Hugh but past him through the window and on to where the lake was visible, gleaming, in the slant of late sunlight. Quietly he said, "I urge you to put it off a while. And think some more."

"About what? My deep roots? It's not like you suppose, Father John. I've already pulled them up, most of them. The rest'll die out pretty soon. And by the way, in case you'd like to know, my wedding day's next Friday." He looked past Father Riley, toward the door. "I'm sorry; I have an appointment now."

Father Riley stood up. "I'll pray for you," he said, "whether you want it or not."

"I appreciate that." He had picked up a sheet of paper but held off looking at it until Father Riley turned away. To his back Hugh said, "Come again, when you feel like having just a friendly talk. I mean that."

So this was it, all Father Riley could do. Out on the street he had walked slowly through the noise and bustle of evening traffic, stopping on the square with his gaze fastened, as by accident, on the time-darkened front of the courthouse and the old-fashioned cupola above. From here, he remembered thinking, it was like the one motionless thing intact in a world that never stopped moving. Illusory, though, a few steps on, when the building's rear extension met his eyes.

He had not gone straight home. He was moved to do what he occasionally did in intervals of agitation: turn west off the square and follow the road that in half a mile mounted up to the long bridge spanning the lake. Partway up was a bench along the rail and he sat gazing out over the water—serene today, limpid blue in last sunlight, the stillness curiously unbroken by the usual squall of motorboats. Across were wooded hills and stretches of bluff, but down a ways the lake fanned out, spread between invisible shores like a vast unruffled ocean. Farmland out there, once, all buried, with its people. There was an odd thing he had only recently learned. Not too many years ago the name of this town was Lorreta, after a woman dear to the old town's history. It had to do with Indians and lives she had saved from a raid. But now, amid much bitter strife, the name had been changed to the present one.

Another small episode of this day, a coincidental one, had stuck in Father Riley's memory. On the way back, pausing in front of the drugstore across from the courthouse, he had started to enter. It was just when a woman, tall and elegant, groomed to perfection, came out the door. Evidently she knew him because, for a mere instant, she hesitated and, face-on, gave him such a look as left him startled. With his gaze he followed her up the sidewalk, trying to determine who she might be and why that look. He was not unaccustomed, especially when wearing his priestly clothes, to curious or suspicious or even hostile eyes turned on him. But not like this, never with an expression of such pure and icy contempt. It was some time before he discovered that she was the woman who now had become Hugh's wife.

3

NORA (Nora Helton still, though remarried) came from a Catholic family in a lower-class suburb of Atlanta. Untypically their immediate neighborhood was almost solid Catholic, with a church, St. Matthews, at the center of it. Her parents were firmly orthodox and careful that Nora and her little sister grow up imbued with all the church's accustomed teachings. Such, at least, was their aim, enforced by proper discipline. They were admirably successful with Annie, who was three years younger than Nora and, understandably, their favorite. For Nora was of a different kind. From about her tenth year she showed signs of rebelliousness, which no doubt drew added impetus from the unequal treatment she received. In such cases normal jealousy is a not an unlikely result, but Nora's jealousy, by-and-by, grew to the level of malice. There were small acts of cruelty toward her sister: hiding or destroying dolls, locking doors against her, threatenings. The result at last was a grimly serious incident, fateful for her as well as for Annie.

It was an accident, Nora insisted, summoning tears besides the real ones inspired by the aftershock. Annie, running to her mother's call, had tripped at the top of the stairs and fallen head over heels down the whole long flight. An accident. But in fact it was Nora's foot that had done it, by an impulse of its own. So she told herself at the time. That Annie never regained half her eyesight was a fact that did not in substance change Nora's untold story. It became, however, her deepest secret, like a worm somewhere in the depths of her, blindly eating away. It was also the beginning of her hatred for priests, who, at the confessions regularly required of her, seemed as if probing for it. "Nothing else, child?" "No, Father." "Only those little sins?" "That's all, Father." To deflect their apparent intentions she came to invent and confess some slightly more serious sins.

By the time she was fourteen her course was set. Already, both at home and at the parochial school taught mostly by priests and nuns, she was paying only lip service to the teachings, religious and otherwise, that she was expected to embrace. To be her own secret self became her motto, of which, despite the isolation it compelled, she was increasingly proud. There were, of course, times when she regretted her isolation and looked about her with an eye for friends of a certain kind. But none appeared, not yet. Out in the world that lay waiting, there would be choices, she thought. Another year, or two at most, and she would be on her way.

Meanwhile, except for the cherished privacy her room afforded, her life at home resembled her life at school. There was much talk of holy things, along with instruction, much prayer (often praying for money), and also the need, though somewhat less of it, for her discretion. But this, discretion, was a practice that as time went on grew ever more difficult. And finally a day came when, at a single stroke, she all but abandoned it. The cause was a priest, Father Parrelli, a fat greasy one she already hated. In a letter he apprised Nora's father of her faults. They were not academic; she was an excellent student. They were spiritual failings: indifference amounting almost to contempt for holy things, abrupt manners, a general reluctance to cooperate. But his centerpiece, enclosed with the letter, was two lines of blasphemous mockery written on a scrap of paper that had somehow found its way into Father Parrelli's hands: "The Lord is my shepherd, but I am not a sheep." If she was to continue in the school, she must show true repentance, a genuine change of heart.

This was the occasion for her father's explosion of wrath, the first ever in her presence. In spite of herself, it moved her to respond in kind, loudly declaring that she was not a sheep and that Father Parrelli, along with the rest, was a hypocritical pig. She went raging out of her father's presence, leaving behind her a fund of ill will that time would barely diminish.

She did, however, burying her contempt, make a show of reformation adequate to keep her in the school for the time still remaining. At home, despite occasional righteous remarks indirectly aimed at her by her father, she kept her mouth shut and stayed as much as possible in her room. Then, unexpectedly, she made a friend, of sorts.

It was something that just happened in the drift of things. Late one evening in a rather shabby and poorly lighted bookstore several blocks from her home he approached and, though she had never seen him before, spoke to her with a certain air of familiarity. He was a little smaller than she but, judging by his confident manner and evident knowledgeableness, several years older. His rather drawn or bitten face did not appeal to her but he was interesting and she was glad enough to have him walk her home in the twilight. He talked all the way, telling her that he lived nearby, that his name was Nick Meagher, that he had once been a Catholic, and that he had been to many cities and also other places she had never heard of. On the sidewalk in front of her house where lights were burning now, he told her he would like to see her again.

It was a friendship to her taste, secret because she knew instinctively that her parents would interfere. In the night she would slip out through her window to meet him. They would walk about through the district, stopping sometimes in front of dim store windows or in a little park where there were benches. But they had a favorite place. It was an alley not far from her house, a place always deserted, where they sat on kegs or upturned buckets, talking. He did most of it but not all. Finally, with a feeling of release that surprised her, she had told him even the deepest of her secrets. He understood. He too had been part of a family once; he too had been forced to suffer in secret the tyranny of priests. Hypocrites, he said, and happened to be reminded of something that made Nora laugh out loud. It was certain knowledge, he said, for he had witnessed it. It was Father Parrelli's nocturnal visits to a brothel on Dandridge street. Meagher knew many things, including some he darkly hinted at. Always there was a point at which he would leave these things unsaid.

Their friendship led to intimacies that never went all the way. She welcomed his hands, cool but with a touch like fire, exploring her body, exciting gusts of a passion she had never felt before. But always that was the end of it; he would stop and leave her panting, mutely urging him on. Each time out she thought again: Tonight is when it will happen.

It was not to be. One night her father discovered her absence and was waiting up when she came home. There was another blowup, questions she would not answer, and angry scenes in the days that followed. Hateful, wicked girl! When finally, throwing discretion to the winds she again went out in the night, she could not find him anywhere. She tried again and then again, but never a trace of him. Until one night she discovered a note somehow there on her pillow. "I have been away and have to go again. But I will be back, to stay. Believe in me . . . M." She hid it away, returning daily to read it over again. It was a long time later before she discovered that she had mislaid it somewhere. Almost bitterly she regretted this, as if the last testimony to his real existence had been taken from her. And this was the more true when she finally realized that, in spite of continuing efforts to do so, she could not with any precision call up a memory of his face.

Her life at home had become practically intolerable. She was turning sixteen and this was the age for which she had been waiting, planning to set out on her own. But now, directly confronting the problems involved, she gave it up. There was, however, one thing she could do: transfer to a public school. Because of her father's flat refusal, in spite of the money it would save, she had to invent a scheme. She soon came up with one, an inspiration that delighted her. Just inside the church, by an exit door that opened toward the school building, was a holy water font. The students on the way to Mass passed it every day, so this was the one she chose. She was ready with her bottle of ink and, right out in the open, she poured until she had turned the water black. The result, as expected, was outrage, and given her already unwholesome reputation, the decision to expel her followed with surprising swiftness. The only thing available to placate her father, a tight-fisted man for good reason, was to remind him again of the money he would save.

It was much better at the public high school: no priests, no Mass, no holy talk. Somehow she had expected that now she would begin to participate in the school's social life and go on dates with boys, but except now and then she did not. Especially where the boys were concerned it would have been easy. By now she had blossomed, grown slimmer in a way that accentuated both her height and the graceful lines of her body, and these along with her rich dark hair and darker eyes made her good to look at. There were times, a few, when she went on dates, and twice when she stooped to indulge herself in what she now mockingly thought of as "the forbidden." She did it with some passion, though she realized that simple defiance had contributed to her pleasure. Indeed, she thought, it might have happened more often had it not been for the lingering memory of those nights in the alley with "him." . . . Would he come back ever? In such moments of doubt she thought of herself as caught in an act of betrayal.

But most of her leisure time she spent in her room studying, determined that she would leave far behind her all, even the memory, of the things she hated so . . . including the penny-pinching. And when, late in her senior year, she received a full scholarship to the state college she was finally certain that she was on her way.

Exactly what she was aiming for was uncertain, but throughout those four years she studied hard to get there. In that whole time she went home only once, for her father's funeral, all the while wondering why. She decided that mainly it was for the purpose of making his death real for her, amounting, as it were, to a guarantee of final liberation. Indeed, as she later observed, it was after this event that she began to emerge from her habit of isolation. Even the memory of "him" was now a receding one. She made friends of a certain kind and went to parties and experienced the warm but transient attentions of two or three zealous boys. But there was only one male to whom, for a while, she would gladly and truly have given herself. He was her philosophy professor, whose rationalist view of all things she labored to make her own. This led to her first and only particular ambition. She would go to graduate school and herself become a professor.

It was not to be realized, though even after graduation the idea lingered in her mind, persisting throughout the year when she was employed as a social worker in the Atlanta slums. During that year she came to be sought after by men of the liberated kind and for once, despite her lingering ambition, was rather enjoying herself. The end of it all concurred with her abrupt separation from the one whose embraces she had been enjoying, at last merely enduring, for a month or so. It had been an interlude much like a long night out interrupted by acts of copulation that with each performance grew less interesting. She remembered best his long hair in her face. Then she found herself not only alone but penniless, the two of them having spent the last coin of all that she had so carefully laid up. Penniless. She hated the word, the memories.

Thoughts of marriage had never been much on her mind, but eight months later she met Wilbur, who took her fancy. Why? Following the birth of her daughter too soon after the marriage, she began to ask herself this question.

She had recognized that Wilbur, though affecting otherwise, was not truly of her kind. It might have been secret maternal longings in her, inspired perhaps by still more deeply suppressed feelings of alienation. When she found herself pregnant she had immediately thought of abortion. In spite of Wilbur's vigorous objection, she made plans to go through with it. But in the end she could not, and so they got married. A mistake, this last. She had misread Wilbur. She had concluded that if he was not quite of her kind he was near enough, and that besides, and now importantly, he was a man qualified to get ahead in the world. Wrong. He was indecisive, given to lengthy spells of bitter dissatisfaction with things in general, obscurely shadowed by a vague nostalgia that, as she was qualified to perceive, had its origin in the obnoxious Catholic religion he had discarded years ago. Moreover she felt that he did not value her or even her lovely daughter to the degree that was their due.

In any case, Wilbur seemed to be going no place. He despised his job at the insurance company where he worked, if without promotion, for four years, and at last decided to quit and enroll in law school, largely delegating to her the business of maintaining the family. He graduated with honors but still was unable to find a position permanent and lucrative enough to support them in the manner rightly expected of him. Get rid of him? She did not. So it went on for years . . . going nowhere. Once more "he," with shrouded face, came back to her at times, a shade on her mind's horizon.

Off and on, idly, Nora continued to think about divorce, to which she had no objection except that inspired by her obsessive concern for her daughter. For it had come to be obsessive, in part because of the child's poor health. At an early age she developed incipient tuberculosis and for some years running lived in the constant threat of that disease. Even when she at last made a full recovery, her health continued to be a dogged concern. So it was that Nora, in spite of her considerable talents, distrusted her ability to provide all she deemed necessary for Jean. Another marriage, someone rich? With luck, maybe, but a risk. Still sticking with tiresome Wilbur, she agreed when finally he proposed that they move to his hometown. There he would start a practice of his own, in a fairly small but progressive place where, he hoped, he still had a few friends. He did not mention his brother, Hugh, with whom he was not congenial and of whom he probably was jealous.

Her original meeting with Hugh did not take place for a couple of days and then was a brief formality. Later, on Hugh's initiative, the brothers established a sort of relationship that amounted to occasional dinners at restaurants ... with Nora, of course, included. These were pleasant enough, though more so for Nora and Hugh who almost from the beginning felt a secret spark between them. It was Nora who first, by the most ambiguous of gestures, let her feelings be known to him. Later, when she discovered that he was a man of real means, she allowed these gestures to clarify themselves. It was slow work because Hugh resisted. In fact, as she discerned, he was shocked. She appeared to back off, playing the game, judging that, most likely, time was on her side. And it was, though drawn out a great deal longer than she had expected. It might have been longer still had it not been for a secret urge that Hugh vaguely deplored in himself. It was to give his brother pain.

Another cause of delay was the fact that the divorce became complicated. Wilbur (out of sheer perversity, she thought) contested it, stoutly and adroitly denying her grounds of neglect and mental cruelty. More, he demanded half-time custody of Nora Jean. This, though with some uneasiness because of her still secret and ongoing affair with Hugh, she fought tooth and nail. It was her daughter's unqualified expression of choice that at last allowed Nora to prevail. Even then, however, the fulfilment of her intention remained at some distance in the future.

This was Hugh's fault, but only, or mainly, because he feared appearances. His success in his law practice (he was city attorney now) and in general had made him respected in the town. He knew he was thought to be untouched by the moral heedlessness that had become all but rampant here as elsewhere, and he shrank from being numbered with the common lot. So for some months, despite his often impassioned desire, he resisted Nora's urgings. It was Nora's growing vexation that finally moved him, before he was yet quite comfortable with the thought, to go ahead and marry.

Now she was married to a man of means in whom she could take pride, whose lavish gifts already were promise of things to come, and for whom she did feel some real affection: with these and her daughter's future now assured, Nora found herself possessed of all she had hoped for. Or nearly so, for a little edge of uneasiness remained. But this would pass; she would charm it away and he would be hers completely. Meanwhile she entered into the life of the town.

She had already learned that there was a great deal of life, or at least of subdued unrest, to enter into. She sometimes thought of the town as Atlanta in microcosm, all its discords and rivalries and hatreds and ambitions crowded together in one diminished space. There were the old natives, fundamentalists mostly, in the minority now, who impotently raged against the town that had come to be. There was a sizable black community given to throes of seething outrage at each new allegation of mistreatment. There were the very rich (the yacht people) and the poor; warlike liberals and conservatives; rebellious gangs with motorcycles who opposed they knew not what. And crime, the rate exceptionally high, most often related to drugs whose dealers and clients conducted their traffic in the virtual shadow of the police station. All this and more. And yet, as she often felt, all this was exciting, was good. A preparation, a meltdown, eating away at the tyranny of traditions that stifled freedom.

It was not long after her marriage that cause for excitement began to register on a more visible scale. Already Nora was part of a small but growing organization called Vistas, whose business it was to trumpet and redress social abuses in the town and county. Now, with the race for mayor getting under way, they were presented with more material means for advancing their causes. There were three candidates, one of whom was a member of Vistas. He was Tad Klein, an urbane Jew of independent means, an abrasively witty man with a challenging razorlike voice. The other two candidates were, as Nora saw it, hopeless. One was the rotund and verbally bumbling owner of the local Chevrolet agency, Norman Baker. The other, Reverend Stark, was a Church of Christ preacher pure and simple ... especially simple, as Nora saw it. But he too had a voice, a high-pitched prophetic voice with an energy that all but compelled attention. He also had God, and all the ground where he stood was holy ground. Nora, compelled on other grounds to stop sometimes and listen to him, gnashed her teeth. "Exterminate" was a word that often crossed her mind.

On a day in June when the campaign was at midpoint, Nora and her daughter were present among the crowd on the town square, on purpose for an event. There was shade of elm and pecan trees on the lawn and on the courthouse steps where the candidates stood. But the lawn was the location most crowded of all, and Nora and Jean had to seek a place for themselves out on the pavement in the hot sun. Standing there in the little pool of isolation the crowd had cleared for them, the pair made a striking picture: except in height a match for one another, in bonnets of blue straw and pale summery garments lightly fitted. Excluding change of facial expressions they scarcely moved at all, just listened, plainly hearing the crescendo of angry voices rudely interrupting one another ... a debate.

The issue, the principal one so far, was the new abortion clinic soon to open its doors. At one point in the verbal melee, "murderer" was among the words the two of them heard. An insult, enraging to Nora, for she herself was among the clinic's promoters. The angry movement of her head deflected her gaze, deflected it just enough to touch and fasten upon a figure not far away. It was that priest, standing in profile to her, in a spatial isolation of his own. Despite the sun's heat, he was in uniform, a slight figure sternly erect, a nose rather large and a little crooked. It was Nora's first real look at him. She saw his head move, a gesture of agreement, and presently, with emphasis, the opposite of agreement. Wrong each way, stupidly, hatefully wrong! New anger lifted her gorge for a moment and she looked away. When she looked back he was gone. To Jean she leaned her head and whispered, "Did you see him ... that priest?"

With lids suddenly lifted, lids heavier than Nora's, she quietly said,

"Yes. I've seen him before." As though from a secret they quickly turned their eyes away from each other.

They stayed on, delighting in Klein's sarcastic jabs, the reverend's sputtering rage at the other's spiteful mockery. At one point God's vengeance was called down, and answered with a taunting grin that for a tense moment looked as if it might be met with the reverend's upraised fist. The moment passed, the fist was withdrawn, but the threat was still there in the fervor of that heraldic voice. The reverend, though much the taller man, was thin to emaciation, and it seemed a wonder that this frail body had strength to command such a voice.

That tense moment between the two men on the steps did pass, but it left a riffling through the crowd. Then more than a riffling, movement around her and a rising babble of voices. It was mostly toward the rear of the crowd where, among parked motorcycles, some black-capped boys appeared to be the center of the disorder. For a little space, still hopeful, she tried to ignore it all. But this became impossible. There were angry cries back there, a teeming of the crowd . . . a fight. Bodies pushed against her. Jean's straw hat was dislodged. A police whistle sounded and louder voices and a shout like a cry of pain. With Jean by the hand she wove her way out, crossed the lawn, hurrying on to the street beyond and the lot where her car was parked.

4

Far more trying for Father Riley than his daily and considerable obligations was his feeling of helplessness. Even in respect to his tiny parish he could not escape the evidence that he was failing. This was clear enough in the fact that on average scarcely two-thirds of his parishioners attended even Sunday mass on a regular basis. For a while, in hopes of attracting the faint of heart, he had added a daily evening mass in addition to the morning one. This made no difference; the result was only that there were more occasions on which he found himself offering Christ's body and blood to an empty church. His passionate homilies, which he prepared with increasing scrupulousness, seemed to move only the few, and his efforts to nourish Christian fellowship by means of such things as picnics were never more than small successes. The nearest thing to gratifying was the continued existence of his classes in church doctrine, which, consisting of both boys and girls, sometimes numbered a dozen or more. He tried not to dwell on the consideration that this success was partly due to parents who wanted the children off their hands. Nevertheless the children were his for some few hours each week. And recently, with unaccustomed guile, he had extended the attraction of his services with offer of an extra hour of supervised playtime in the yard behind the church.

Was it this way everywhere, the church shrinking, speaking to ears gone nearly deaf, resorting to petty stratagems like this one of his own? There had been a day not long ago when its great voice was heard, condemning evils, standing out with force in public against the world's obscenities. Like abortion, accepted now, soon to be made in this small town a worthy institution. Was his the lone voice daily and with passion upraised to heaven in defense of all those innocent ones ripped from their mothers' wombs? Or so it had seemed to him, more and more ... up until yesterday. A strange ally, that preacher.

Father Riley was reluctant. Fundamentalists, though often doctrinally sound, in general tried his patience. But his long hours of self-questioning left him with the certainty that it was his duty, and shortly after noontime he was in his car and on the way.

The preacher's church was on this side of town, half a mile or so out the Rainsville road, and he soon found himself approaching the squat white-painted frame building whose sign out front said, blatantly to Father Riley, Church of Christ. Close next door was a small residence, surely the manse, with an extension on the church side that Father Riley took to be the preacher's office. He was right, his knock awakened footsteps, and the opening door revealed the tall emaciated figure of Reverend Stark. The astonishment in his face was no real surprise, and Father Riley said, "Could I talk to you about something?" The astonishment remained, but after a pause the door was opened for him.

Inside, the heat was scarcely diminished. Through the big west window the midday sun detailed books on shelves and a ragged stack of magazines and pamphlets on the desk behind which the reverend had already seated himself. On the wall behind him was a calendar picture of Jesus knocking at the gate, on which Father Riley's eyes rested in a moment of hesitation.

"Set down if you want to."

The gaunt face, curious, less than friendly, looked straight at him. Father Riley sat down in a sternly upright, wooden chair, preparing words. The reverend preceded him:

"You're the Catholic priest, huh ... with your collar. I seen you around."

"Yes." Then, after a pause, "I know you don't approve of the Catholic Church, but there are a lot of things we agree about. Abortion's one. We consider it murder, infanticide, just like you." A faint stiff nod was his answer, and he went on. "I was thinking we could join hands ... just in this one thing."

"Doing what?" He had not removed his challenging gaze from Father Riley's face.

"Protesting it. The new clinic. I thought if we could gather..."

"That's just exactly the thing our church aims to do," the reverend interrupted. "We're going to let them know. Stop it if we can... in God's own name."

"I'm glad to hear that," Father Riley said. "If we..."

"But I tell you straight out, Mr. Priest, it ain't going to be any joining hands. You do your business and we'll do ours. I'm sorry but that's how we believe; we're a Bible religion. It ain't any true word but the Word of God in that Bible." His eyes had opened a little wider and there was the hint of a spark in them. In some discomfort Father Riley blinked and might have got up except for the voice coming at him again.

"I reckon you try to be a good man in that church of yours, if you can call it that, but God's Word is square against you. He made it plain. You look in the Book of Revelation, what it says about the Whore of Babylon. And idols in your church. Look anywhere in the Bible. Just read and see. It looks mighty like you're serving the devil instead of Jesus Christ."

Father Riley stood up. Except "I'm sorry you think those things," he made no reply as he turned to the door and left.

During the drive back, Father Riley managed to suppress his indignation. After all it was not malice but only ignorance, blighting ignorance. But reflection led him to a thought that angered him for a different reason. At least this half-literate country parson could speak for his congregation as he, Father Riley, could not speak for his. And doubtless this parson with his flock in hand would be conspicuously there when the clinic's doors opened on Monday morning.

Father Riley parked his car and went straight into the chapel by the back door. At the little shrine of the Virgin he knelt and prayed, "Hail Mary," over and over again. "Pray for us sinners now, and at the hour of our death." But there was something wrong: he was seeing himself. He was an outsider looking in on a man doing a strange thing, on his knees muttering the same words time after time to an inanimate statue. That was how it looked, through that preacher's eyes, through everybody's eyes, as from a world as alien as planets to each other. He would not submit. He shook it off and prayed a while longer and got onto his feet with resolution firm in his mind.

Next morning at Sunday mass he entered the pulpit with that same resolution and delivered the homily that he had so scrupulously prepared the night before. He was mindful but did not care that the faces, the familiar two-thirds, looked back at him with a sort of stricken attention. He soon recognized in his own voice the note of accusation and again did not care but only cared that his words should have the strength to move, to shame them in the light of the holy faith they professed. He spoke of the innocent little ones torn from their mothers' bodies, an act as brutal as Herod's murders multiplied by thousands; of indifference certain to spread like disease through society at large. Think what must surely follow, he said, when the mantle of the sacred no longer was there to shelter human life. What then for the very old, for the halt, for all the ones deemed finally useless to themselves and society? And what of God and His wrath, Who had made it plain that He would not withhold His hand forever?

After these words Father Riley stood there in the pulpit for a silent moment before he said, lest it not be plain enough already, "I will be there tomorrow morning, at nine o'clock, in front of the clinic. To protest, with restraint, in the name of Christ and His church, this terrible thing. I hope you will be there . . . all of you." For one more silent moment he stood looking into their faces. They did or did not look back at him, with expressions that told him nothing.

ॐ ॐ ॐ

The clinic, just outside the business district, was a renovated residence house, newly bricked, with an expansive oak tree in the front yard. Divided by the walkway, a small but growing crowd was on hand, including two policemen. Nora, bonneted against the heat, and Hugh were there, standing well back from the sidewalk in the shade of the tree. Like most of the crowd they were quiet for the moment. Until Nora said, "Look who's coming," and pointed.

"I was afraid of that," Hugh said, watching Father Riley approach, accompanied by a woman and an old man with a cane.

"At least he's not carrying a sign saying 'Murderers,'" Nora dryly said.

"Oh, he'll behave himself. Maybe just deliver a few holy words," Hugh replied.

But in that same moment they both saw just such a sign approaching, upheld above a considerable body of people, men and women, some of whom also carried signs. At the foot of the sidewalk they stopped and for a minute or two, like the people already assembled, stood in silence.

"That goddamn preacher," Nora murmured.

"Anyway the good Father's not one of them, thank God."

Nora gave him a glance.

Then there were voices, swelling into a hymn, "Rock of Ages," led by Reverend Stark from under his swaying sign that said "Baby Killers." But now there was competition, boos and razzing from some of the crowd close around Nora and Hugh, a cacophony of rival voices growing louder and louder. With force enough to be heard, Nora said, "What a stupid, stupid mess."

Suddenly the voices fell away and among the crowd behind Reverend Stark a policeman was trying to open a path. With him were two women wearing hats that all but concealed their faces. The policeman was giving loud orders, pushing people aside, making at least slow progress until he came face-to-face with Reverend Stark. Quite audibly the policeman's voice carried over the crowd. "Step out the way, Reverend." But the reverend stood his ground and, uplifting that prophetic voice, cried, "In the name of Jesus Christ we will not . . ."

"Get out the way, Reverend!" At this one's side another policeman appeared and took the reverend by the arm. Instantly Reverend Stark broke free and lifted his right hand at arm's length in the air as though to signal the oncoming of a heaven-sent proclamation. But what seemed to be the direct result was something else: a ripple through the crowd and voices raised and suddenly a missile in the air.

"Oh my God," Nora said. Quickly Hugh seized her arm and drew her back into the protection of the tree trunk. This took no more than a second or two, but somehow it was time enough for disorder to become violence, with bodies shoving and mingled angry shouts and again a missile, more than one, rocks seemingly thrown at random. Someone was on the ground, underfoot, it seemed, and before the police whistles began to sound and policemen with busy nightsticks penetrated the crowd, there were more victims than one struggling to stand up.

Well beyond the tree trunk now, Nora said, "Don't be a fool. Come on," because Hugh had suddenly stopped.

"Wait a minute."

"Why?"

Hugh did not answer. He was staring into the crowd, a crowd now ceasing to be a mob, beginning to disperse. "Stay here," he said and went striding away back into the dying melee. It was the priest, Nora saw, that damned priest. He was standing alone, with a bloody head, looking as if he did not know which way was left or right. Hugh had him by the arm, was urging him, was leading him back toward her. Close now, he was gently saying to him, "You need a doctor for that. I'll get my car."

"No," the priest said. "I'm all right." With his fingers he was wiping blood from his eye. There was blood on his collar too.

To Nora, Hugh said, "Haven't you got something in your purse . . . Kleenex?"

She shook her head. "No."

"Please look."

Quite deliberately she opened the purse swung at her hip and pretended to look inside.

"Never mind," Father Riley said. "I'm all right; it's just a short walk." He removed Hugh's hand from his arm and, pausing to say "Thank you," a little unsteadily turned away.

"Okay," Hugh said. "We'll walk along with you."

"I'll go on home," Nora said.

Hugh looked back at her. With a flicker of anger he said, "It wouldn't hurt you to come along. You might be able to help."

She met him eye for eye, a moment of defiance. Then, Why not? she thought, and faintly nodded, and followed a little behind them.

Between the chapel and the priest's quarters out back was a fenced-in area where a few children were playing on a swing and a slide and a seesaw. As one they stopped, fell silent, looking with wide eyes at Father Riley.

Old Mrs. Gallagher, overseeing in his place, got up from her chair with a suddenness that made her stagger. "Oh Lord, I was afraid of something," she cried, and came to him and took his arm. "A wicked world it is."

"It's all right," he said. "Just a little scalp wound. You know how they bleed."

She led him, with lamentations, to the door of his quarters and inside, and Hugh followed. Nora stayed where she was.

Still standing there she observed the children, all of whose eyes were on her.

"He'll be fine," she said to them and watched as they returned, hesitant and almost wordless now, to their play. There were seven of them, ranging in age from a boy of about six to a rather husky but pretty girl who might have been nine or ten. After a few moments she noticed that the girl had tearstains on her face. Devoted little follower, Nora thought, no doubt with a brain already pickled in ancient superstition.

Nora turned and looked at the chapel. Of course she had seen it before and had to admit that as a building, with its white-washed walls, arched and stained glass windows, and gracefully truncated steeple, it was not without charm. But this was not what moved her to go inside. She entered by the back door and once beyond the chancel stopped for a view of the whole interior. Here it was: deceptive tinted light from the pictured windows, burning candles, embossed or painted figures from that vast panoply of myth; there the plaster Virgin sorrowing in her grotto; and high up, commanding all, the storied Victim stretched on his miserable cross. All this, even today, making victims in His stead of the many who never could erase its stamp from their minds and hearts.

Remembering an appointment, she left the chapel. The children were hard at play again, except for that oldest girl, who was not with them. Nora crossed the yard to the open door and looked in for Hugh. He was not in sight, neither he nor the woman. But the priest was there, clean of face and bandaged, half propped up on a sofa. On the floor beside him, holding his hand and looking up at him with an air of rapture, was the girl. Nora stood gazing. Soon, from somewhere out of view, she faintly heard Hugh's voice. She turned and passed the children by and waited for him in the maple shade beside the chapel.

≥● ≥● ≥●

With silence between them Hugh drove slowly past the clinic. All was quiet, the yard deserted except for two policemen. Three blocks on and he stopped in front of the beauty parlor at the corner of the square. With a murmured word on his part only, he let Nora off and drove to his office where he was late for a meeting with a client. He spent most of the day in and out of the courthouse, observing on the side that this morning's uproar had made no visible difference in the daily business of the town. But he was curious, and when he finally left his office that evening and walked to where his car was parked, he had the luck to see the police chief, Dan Bostick, coming down the courthouse steps. Hugh hailed him.

It turned out to be a lengthy conversation, so that finally they sat down on one of the lawn benches. The morning's consequences? Six had been arrested, including Preacher Stark and four young men from his congregation. Two were charged with assault and the others with resisting an officer. All except the one not a member of Stark's church were already out on bail.

"That old fool," the chief said. "Plenty old enough to know better." In fact he was not as old as the chief himself, who had been chief once in the past and had been temporarily reappointed when, a month ago, the then-current chief was fired because one of his officers, in much-questioned circumstances, had killed a black man. Hugh had known Dan Bostick since the days when this old man was still lean and quick of hand and his head did not have a tremor whenever he looked directly at someone.

"Running for mayor, by God," the chief went on. "What a bunch. I wish Stacy had put in again; he handled it better than most of them have. Bunch of fools. I'll be glad when it's over, though."

Hugh started to defend Tad Klein, but settled for a noncommittal nod.

"There's plenty of fools besides them in this town, though," the chief added. "Worse than fools. Go off like firecrackers. Like they're ready to turn on you for just about nothing. I never in my life saw as much bad feeling as is here between the different kinds. Downright hate each other. Back in old Loretta days, you didn't have to hit them in the head with a stick to get their attention." He took off his policeman's cap and looked into it as though for some kind of an answer.

"A changing world," Hugh said. "Just that it came on us so fast. It'll work itself out, though, just needs a while to do it. And look at the good things it's brought us already. Look at this town."

"Yeah, I see it," the chief said, still looking into his cap.

"When I was a boy it was next to nothing. I would have left here as soon as I got grown, just to make a decent living."

"Well," the chief said. "All the same I wish some of those old bad things could come back. Before all these people kill each other."

"Cheer up, Chief, maybe they won't." Hugh got up and touched the old man's shoulder and went on to his car.

5

Approaching his front door Hugh could already hear the familiar music. It was *Swan Lake*; Jean was dancing. He closed the screen softly behind him and stole his way to the wide door that opened into the den. There she was, graceful in tights and ballet slippers, bent to the horizontal, with long white arms and one sheer leg outstretched; then erect in one smooth motion, her lithe body turning, turning full circle. Then she saw him, and froze.

"Don't stop," he said. "You were doing beautifully."

Her response was only to say, "I'm through, anyway," and walk to the corner and switch the tape player off. She quickly put the throw rugs back in place, opened the drapes, and left through the door to the dining room.

It was typical. In all these months he had made no progress with her. It was small consolation that, apparently, she was not much less unfriendly toward her father.

"The Blankenships are due in a few minutes."

It was Nora's voice, from behind him, as she passed on into the dining room and through to the kitchen at the back of the house. Also less than friendly, he thought, recalling her silence in the car this morning. It vexed him. His sympathy for poor Father Riley was only human, and not, as she should know, a sign that he was backsliding. He turned his thoughts elsewhere, to the Blankenships.

He was not pleased with this thought, either. Ralph Blankenship, for more reasons than one, was not his favorite person. But this was necessary, a social obligation already much overdue. Besides, it was something less than prudent to neglect such friendship as he had with a man of

Blankenship's wealth and standing in the town. Real estate, of which Blankenship was Lakepoint czar, was, as Hugh reflected, the way to go in these times.

When, a bit refreshed, he came downstairs, the Blankenships were already present, seated in the spacious fir-paneled den, graciously ready to accept Hugh's excuse for his tardiness. While Hugh served drinks from the little glass-topped table (Scotch for him, gin and tonic for her) Ralph was already in verbal high gear. It was his new boat, that had cost him eighty-five thousand. "But it was worth it, Hugh, every bit," he said. "Two hundred and twenty horse inboard engine, fast as an automobile. Cabin with all the comforts of home. You'll have to come for a trip with us, it'll carry us anywhere. New Orleans if we took the notion." He was an athletic-looking man, much too big for his current wife, Annie, who lived as in his shadow, nodding in all but perpetual affirmation of his words. He had a way of looking very directly into the faces of his auditors, to drive his words home, and in this case more and more the face was Nora's. Hugh did not wonder; the beauty parlor had done something special with her hair, sweeping it back, making its darkness appear almost blue. But if he did not wonder, he was nevertheless put off by that fixed gaze of Ralph's. That the man had a reputation was not the cause. It was simply that voracious look in his eyes. By force Hugh changed the subject to that morning's uproar at the clinic.

"Goddamn preacher. He ought to be strung up," Ralph said. "We've got enough troubles in this town without fanatics like that one. Jesus!"

"I hope that'll be the end of it," Hugh said.

Annie gave a hopeful nod, but Ralph said, "I doubt it. Holy Joes like that don't give up easy. Of course that Catholic priest was in it too." He hesitated. "You're not still one of them, are you . . . Catholics?"

"No," Hugh blandly said. "I just grew up in it." He glanced at Nora who merely sat there quietly with an alert expression on her face. "But I saw the light," he added.

"A good thing, too. I've been reading in the newspaper about Catholics. Priests, I mean. All their sex doings. One was even a bishop. Went for children. 'Course it's no wonder, they won't let them have wives. You can't trust them."

"I don't think that's very common," Hugh said. "Most of them are good people." He glanced at Nora again. She was listening intently.

"Well, enough of them's not. I wouldn't want to trust them. Besides all that hokum about saints and magic medals and such. People in their right minds got past that kind of thing five hundred years ago."

It was only because of Nora that Hugh was able to keep his vexation from showing. Still he rather abruptly said, "Well, I hope there's no more trouble about the clinic. It's something we've been needing here. To stop that back-alley stuff."

Ralph seemed a bit reluctant to drop the subject of Catholics but, to the evident relief of his wife, he went along with Hugh. "You're right about needing it," Ralph said, reaching for the bottle of Scotch. "But like I said, I kind of doubt the trouble's all over. One thing's that nigger boy."

"What boy?" Hugh said.

"The one they took to jail. They say he was hurt enough so they had to halfway carry him off. Cop hit him with his stick."

"Oh my God," Nora quietly said, almost the first words Hugh had heard her speak.

"Yeah," Ralph went on. "You know how they are out there, those niggers. And already boiling about that one the cop killed a month ago. More bad news."

This, Hugh recalled, was something that Dan Bostick, a while ago on the courthouse lawn, had failed to mention. "Are you sure about that?"

"Red Walker told me. He saw it, I think." Ralph took a long swallow from his glass, and it seemed as though this was what gave him the inspiration to come out with an ill-considered attempt at humor. "It might maybe be something to interest your brother Wilbur. He goes for this kind of cases, don't he?"

Immediately after, even Ralph saw that he, depending on his knowledge of the brothers' relationship, had stepped over the line. "No offense meant," he lamely said. "None of my business."

But it was enough to leave a damper that shortened the Blankenships' visit, which ended with plainly awkward goodbye words. Hugh, after the door was shut, said, "Lout," and nothing else.

The fact that in the wake of their departure he took it on himself to set things back in order was still not enough to break through Nora's silence. Finally, in the radiant white kitchen, she at the sink with her back to him, he abruptly said, "Are you still mad because I helped him back to the church? It's unreasonable. I'd have done the same for any old acquaintance." When she did not immediately answer, he added, "Do you think I'm in love with him or something? Or is it just my 'reverting,' as you say?"

"Not exactly," she murmured.

"What would 'exactly' mean?"

"Oh, it's mostly the mood I'm in. That business upset me . . . Please hand me those saucers over there."

He settled for this, handing her the saucers, and finally said, "Look, I want to go downtown for a few minutes, to check on what Blankenship said. Maybe when I get home I can persuade you that I'm not 'reverting.'"

"That would be nice," she cooly said.

≈ ≈ ≈

Nora finished in the kitchen and went upstairs to their bedroom. She sat on the edge of the bed for a few minutes, thinking. Then she went down the hall to Jean's room at the far corner of the house. No need to knock, they were that intimate, and she found Jean propped up in bed, in pajamas, reading *Dance* magazine. As expected she smiled at her mother. "I was afraid you wouldn't come for our visit," she said and let the magazine slip onto the floor. Such a pretty girl, Nora thought, very like Nora herself, as people said: eyes, though heavier lidded, the same dark color; hair to match; nose just a trifle prominent, and chin with a shallow cleft. Height was the notable difference, though she might yet grow a little.

Nora sat down on the bed and took her hand. She said, "Is Mr. Needham still giving you compliments?"

"Yes." The smile came back. "The last three lessons. He told me I was the most graceful pupil he ever taught."

"I knew that already," Nora said, squeezing her hand. "Who knows? You might turn out to be an important ballerina."

"I'd like that." The smile faded. "My friends wouldn't, though. All they like is to go out to the pavilion and jump around to rock music."

"You shouldn't care. Not at all. I don't like for you to go out there, anyway. It's not your kind of place."

"I didn't know you minded," Jean said, looking serious. "I won't if you don't want me to."

Nora gave her hand another squeeze. It was time now for her main purpose. "Will you tell me something, dear?" She just paused for Jean's assent. "You know that Catholic priest? You've seen him around . . . with the collar and all."

"Yes. He came to our school, once. And gave a little talk, he and some other preachers. They were all boring."

"Have you ever heard anything about him? From your friends, or anybody?"

She hesitated. "I can't remember."

"Try. Anything not very nice. Anything ugly."

She tried for a moment. "I don't think so."

"Well, would you do something for me. Ask your friends. Anything about him and children, little girls. You know what I mean. Ugly things. I wish you would. We need to know."

Jean's troubled face said that she understood.

"Will you? For me?"

"All right, Mama. I promise."

Nora pressed her hand again and let it go. She leaned and kissed her daughter's forehead and stood up. "Remember," she said, and then, "Good night. I'll see you in the morning."

She went back up to her bedroom and sat on the bed waiting without wishing for Hugh's return.

6

It was late afternoon of the day following the incident at the clinic when Father Riley first heard the news. His persistent headache had sent him to the drugstore, and he had quickly tuned in on a conversation passing between the man in front of him and the clerk behind the counter. Of the people arrested, one was a black boy named Quals, who apparently had taken a more serious lick on the head than Father Riley had. In fact it was enough so that, in the evening, they had removed him from his jail cell out to the regional hospital where, supposedly under guard, he was to stay all night. But he did not stay. During the night he somehow managed to slip out, and not only that but simply vanish. At least the police could not find him and neither, by their claim, could anybody in the black community. But the bad part was that the blacks were suspicious, already muttering about police brutality and that recent "murder," as they called it, of the black man.

"Police better come up with that boy," the clerk said. "Else they'll be out in the streets again. Maybe worse, this time."

"That's for sure," the other man said and left the store.

The clerk was eyeing Father Riley, focusing mainly on his bandaged head. But he said nothing, and Father Riley made his purchase and went out onto the busy street. There he stopped and stood thinking.

He stood there for several minutes, considering, a little wary of the decision he was preparing to take. Then he set out for the police station.

Chief Bostick was there, in a small office at the back of a large room furnished only with a desk and one tired policeman and benches on which several disconsolate-looking people, black and white, were seated. The chief, with his tremulous gaze, regarded him for a moment without speaking. "Help you, sir?"

Father Riley put hesitation aside. "I'd like to know for sure, about that black boy... Quals, isn't it?" The chief's noncommittal nod failed to reassure him, but he went on. "Please don't think I'm assuming anything against the police. I was just wondering why he would vanish like that... if he really did... if they're not just hiding him. I know how it is."

"How what is?" the chief said laconically.

"That they distrust the police... justified or not. It's mostly your business, I know, but it worries me. It might be a lot worse, this time."

The chief leaned back in his chair and, still laconic, said, "Well, sir, it worries me too, but I can't help you. They might be hiding him and they might not. Could of just run away scared. But I can tell you he's got no reason the police gave him. Nothing been done to him but hit him a little harder than was needed in that mess down there yesterday. I hope you'll believe that."

Father Riley could not tell whether the nod he gave was convincing. "I was just thinking I might be able to help. I know the big man out there, Cap Waters. I believe he trusts me. I believe he'd tell me the truth."

It was the chief's head and not his eyes that had the tremor. In the moment before he spoke they appeared to be fastened on Father Riley's bandage. "Maybe. I don't know it'd hurt anything, you being a outsider. Might, might not. But things happen out there. Troubles a heap worse than what's under that bandage of yours. Cap Waters is a hard one to figure."

"I'm willing to risk it."

There was an interruption, sounds of a scuffle out behind him. With a muttered oath the chief got up and went into the big room where two policemen were trying to subdue a drunk, a Mexican struggling and loudly babbling in Spanish. In the moment when Father Riley appeared in the office doorway the Mexican saw him and cried out, "Padre! Padre!" and then, "Me salve! Me salve, Padre!"

Father Riley, defying impulse, held his ground and kept standing there until he felt as sure as he could that nothing but proper restraint was being used. "I'll go on now," he said to the chief, but after a few steps he paused and turned aside and, on the instantly motionless head of the Mexican, put his blessing. The sound of quiet laughter followed him out the door.

The black section was a southeast extension of the town, lying mainly in a broad valley with gradual slopes on either side. Most of the houses were small, a good many of these ramshackle, but on one street, Father Riley's destination, the houses were of moderate size and fairly new. He remembered because he had been here several times in the past, but now in the dimness of late twilight everything seemed strange to him. Few lights in houses were burning, and the people he saw, in front yards and faintly limned on porches, watched without sound or gesture as he passed by. But after a time he recognized the street. The house was third on his right and, approaching, he saw a figure standing at the foot of the porch steps. From the size of the man he knew it was Cap Waters. At the gate he said, "Mr. Waters, it's Father Riley."

"Thought it was." The voice was deep, deep as a voice echoed in a well. "Not many whites come in here these days after daylight."

"Can I talk to you?"

"All right."

Cap sat down on a porch step and, indicating the space beside him for Father Riley, said, "Bet I ain't wrong thinking why you come here."

"You're not," Father Riley said. "It's that boy. Quals." A strange quiet was all around them. Here on the step beside Cap Waters, child-size was how he felt.

"Well," Cap said, "We don't know yet. Not for sure. But it's mighty funny when a black boy runs off like that and nobody got even a notion where he gone. None of 'us,' anyhow."

"I hope you'll give it time enough. Before you do anything."

"Yeah. Time. We good at waiting. Been waiting three hun'erd years."

"I know. But you don't want to make a mistake on this. Set things back again."

"Oh, we'll wait a while. It won't be long 'fore we know. But I tell you, Father, we put up with all the shit we going to take. Fact is, police just plain murdered poor old Tom Wilks . . . and him with a wife and a houseful of chi'ren. I was in Atlanta a long time 'fore I come back here. I seen how black people got right down head-on to the business there. No more shit. Naw, our time out on the streets three weeks ago wasn't nothing. Ain't going be 'nothing' this time. If things get tore up and people gets hurt, it's just what Whitey's got coming . . . 'Course I don't mean you. I figure you for a friend."

Father Riley listened to the silence. Finally he said, "I'm asking you as a friend to please wait till you're really sure, till you've got proof. I talked to Chief Bostick. He swears the police didn't do anything . . . except in that mess at the clinic, like in a fight. I took a little lick, myself. I kind of trust the old man."

"Don't. He's a old-timer. Tell me, back when he was chief before, all kind of ugly stuff went on. And never no payback. Naw. Anyhow, Sim Quals wasn't doing a thing down there but standing there watching. All the police saw was a nigger's head waiting for a nightstick."

In a silence still more ominous now, Father Riley tried to think. "Look," he finally said. "Let's try something. Let me go talk to Mayor Stacey. Both of us, would be better. Put pressure on him. Maybe make him see about putting you, or some black man, on the city council. They say he's pretty reasonable. And Tad Klein would help. He . . ."

"Ain't going to no mayor. He can come to me. It's past time one of them did. And Tad Klein. He ain't nothing but all mouth. You do what you want to. But do it quick."

Father Riley could think of nothing else except to say, "I will," and quietly leave, walking at a measured pace between rows of dimly lit houses where, it seemed to him, invisible and unfriendly eyes followed him all the way.

Tired when he got home, he nevertheless went into the chapel and, on his knees at the altar, prayed for a while. He prayed for the whole world but mainly he prayed for this town where more and more the golden rule seemed to be "Hate Thy Neighbor." But he must do what he could, and he prayed again that God might grant him success in his plan for the morning.

It was not to be. He did not find it difficult to get access to the mayor's office and to Mayor Stacy himself, who at least was knowing and respectful enough to call him Father. This was small consolation, though. He had barely got seated in the offered chair and started into his overture when the dour face beyond the desk hardened with vexation. No, more than vexation; it was anger plain and simple. It was equally clear in the voice that interrupted him. "I've had all I mean to take of Cap Waters. Put him on the city council? That'd take an election anyhow. I'd rather see a mad dog on it. That's one bad nigger and you can't believe a thing he says. Hates white people, and that's the end of it. Just wants trouble. What he'd like best is to see us all dead."

Without any real hope Father Riley said, "But can't something be done? To head off a riot. Maybe a tragic one. I don't believe he's as unreasonable as you think. I know him."

"Well I do too. From a lot more experience with him than you've got." Mayor Stacy, now leaning slightly back in his chair, with the fingertips of both hands pressed tightly together, went on, "I'll tell you what can be done. We can get the National Guard in here if we have to. But the best thing is to find that black boy. He's not any deader than I am, and I'd bet you a pile Cap Waters knows it. Probably knows where he is. Cap's 'spade in the hole.'" He allowed himself a little twitch of a grin at his own humor. But he was not yet finished, and Father Riley, instead of getting up, decided to stay for it.

"But I'm going to tell you something, Father. You're a man of religion and I know you mean to do the right thing. But you're out of your depth, here, and you're mighty likely to do more harm than good. So I ask you to keep your nose out of it. Which is for your own good, too. There's people in this town, lots of them, that wouldn't take kindly to any white man consorting around with such as Cap Waters . . . specially in these days. And I've got to add, hoping not to give offense, specially somebody like you . . . in a collar."

"Thank you," Father Riley said with only a shade of sarcasm, and stood up. "I'll consider your advice," he added, and left the mayor's office and the city hall behind him.

7

Four days after the Quals boy's disappearance, without any notice in the *Lakepoint Herald*, it became known by word of mouth that Cap Waters would make a public statement on the square in front of the courthouse. That this news was able to draw a large crowd of whites as well as some blacks measured the extent of emotion aroused by events of these past few days. The vandalism had consisted not only of store windows and car windshields pointlessly shattered but also two cases of what clearly was arson. One was a shop, a frame structure isolated from other buildings. The other was the Bethel Church of Christ, the Reverend Stark's church, which had been partly saved by Stark's own furious efforts. The Reverend himself was to be seen among the crowd, waiting, with singed unruly hair and a demeanor that vividly proclaimed his unrelenting fury. But so far no arrests, nor even any leads.

Hugh and Nora were there, positioned, along with a few others, on the lawn facing the crowd still gathering out in the street. Exactly at the announced hour, five o'clock, Waters, a head taller than the crowd that opened to let him pass, approached the steps onto the courthouse walkway. Two black men and two black women followed close at his heels, and behind these came a small cluster of whites, several of whom had cameras.

"Reporters, by God," Hugh quietly said. "Probably from Atlanta. The cagey rascal called them here." Nora said nothing, just watched from under the straw bonnet that shaded only half her face from the sun's hot slanting light.

In a sudden quietness of the crowd, Waters, with only the black section of his entourage, mounted the steps and for a long moment stood there as if not even conscious of all the eyes trained on him. He wore no hat. On his shirt, a black T-shirt stretched by the width of his shoulders, in white letters back and front was the word POWER.

An angry voice came out of the crowd. "Who started the fires? You know, don't you?"

Turning heads directed Waters's gaze to a tall man back toward the rear. Quite deliberately, his bass voice needing no amplification, Waters said, "Can't tell you, white man. Could of been you, for all I know. You people got a way of blaming blacks for your own doings." He barely paused. "But that ain't why I come here. I'm here to tell you something." Camera bulbs were flashing. "Our boy Quals is dead. Kilt by police. Got a witness right here." He turned to one of the black women, the big one in a pulled-down hat who, though appearing a little frightened, nodded with emphasis. "She seen it plain. Up there at Cooper's Point. Throwed him in the lake." There was a stirring in the crowd, angry challenging voices. "It's a plain fact, just like it's a plain fact they killed poor old Wilks. And I'm here to tell you . . ."

"Lying bastard," Hugh said. "He's cooked it up. Gutsy, though." But Nora, deaf to his words, was not even looking at Waters. There was a new figure, lately arrived, standing with the little group of blacks behind him. After a moment she said, "There's your priest."

"I see him. The fool! What does he think he's doing?"

Waters's voice, demanding, threatening (something about the police force and trouble to come and seats on the city council, about the power he would summon from Atlanta and other places) was all but failing to register now in Nora's consciousness. Her eyes were on the priest, observing the small bodily gestures that signaled his concurrence, thinking: These would be noticed, remembered . . . enough perhaps to bring him down. So again she listened to the words, with a sort of double pleasure now, thinking how they worked to achieve both her social and personal wishes.

But the words came to a stop. The stirring and angry voices had risen to a threat, and suddenly there were police, a line of them poised between the steps and the shifting crowd beyond. Cap Waters, unfazed, followed by his little contingent, of which the priest was one, amid a flashing of camera bulbs, descended the steps like a conqueror and, escorted, passed through a gap in the crowd.

"How about that?" It was Tad Klein, standing behind them, a half smile on his vaguely equine face. His gaze still followed the little group, with its trailing escort of police and several eager reporters. At the far corner of the square a car was waiting for them. Klein said, "That was guts, wasn't it? Right here in the lion's mouth." He looked at the buzzing crowd, now starting to disperse, except for clusters here and there standing head-to-head. "Where did the priest go?"

"I don't know," Hugh said. "Back to his church."

"That took courage, too."

"And foolhardiness," Hugh said. "Even as it is, he hasn't got much of a congregation." Then, "And what if that's a lie, about the witness. Where's any real evidence?"

"I believe him," Klein said. "I can believe anything about our police force. Maybe this will change things, finally, I hope." Expecting agreement, he looked at Nora, only to be disappointed. In fact it was plain that she was not even paying attention. Her gaze was elsewhere, roving, searching the street out there. When after a moment their silence did catch her attention, she only looked at Hugh and said, "We might as well go home now."

Hugh drove her home but, pretending that he had neglected a small matter at his office, stopped at the front gate to let her out. Nora said, "Why can't it wait till tomorrow, if it's so small?"

"I just want to get it out of the way. I'll be back for supper."

She looked at him, reading him. He should have come up with a stronger excuse, and he hesitated. But she turned away, through the gate and up the walk. Though hesitant still, he went ahead.

He parked in the lot beside the chapel and walked to the door of the quarters out back. His knock brought no answer and, at a venture, he tried the back door of the chapel. It was not locked. He stepped inside . . . into light from his childhood: a wash of tinted sunset rays through the many-colored windows. And young David up there with his harp, Moses and the burning bush, Christ ascending to heaven. He blinked to clear his mind and stepping past the chancel saw to his right, where candles burned and the Virgin stood with sorrowful head bowed down, Father Riley on his knees. Hugh waited, a part of all this silence.

Father Riley got onto his feet and, turning, gave a start. "Hugh," he quietly said.

"I'd like to talk to you, Father John."

"Sure."

He stepped to the nearby pew and sat down. Hugh, at a little distance, joined him, regretting the expectant look on Father Riley's face. But his mind was clear now. "I'm afraid it's not what you're hoping. It's about what happened up there, with Waters. I'm pretty sure he's lying. Using that black woman. He probably convinced her she saw it."

The expectant look was gone, but Father Riley continued to regard him brightly. "I don't believe that. I know Cap Waters. I trust him."

"Well, don't. He's a fanatic. I've seen and heard about too much of this sort of thing. It's possible he believes it really happened, but he hasn't got any proof a court of law would recognize. You're sticking your neck out. These are bad times."

Father Riley looked away, looked up toward the crucifix on the wall in back of the altar. For a long moment the perfect silence seemed to gather around them. He said, "I'm sorry, Hugh. My heart tells me I'm right. Those people have suffered too long. It's my duty, no matter what. But I'm not worried that anything will happen to me."

That innocent face. Aged thirty years? was the question that in this moment flickered across Hugh's mind; half that age might describe it better. He said, "Maybe not. But think about your parishioners, for one thing. Not that it's mainly your safety they'll worry about. It's you being a troublemaker. You represent them." Hugh hesitated. "Unless I'm mistaken, they're not like the old people, faithful to the end . . . enduring all things." In a muted voice he added, "I'm afraid they're more like me. It's the way it is now."

Father Riley's face had fallen. It was an older face, sad. Finally he said, "I'll have to risk it." Then, brightening a little, "I appreciate your concern, though. I'm surprised."

"I am too. But you're welcome."

This pause was longer still, but at last, prefaced by a blinking of his clear gray eyes, Father Riley said, "Do I dare hope you've had second thoughts?"

Hugh could only shake his head, slowly, gravely. He looked away and stood up. "I hope you'll think about what I said. And other things, too, maybe."

"I will. And come to see me again."

Hugh gave him a nod, and left.

Nora and Jean were eating in the kitchen, already near the end of their meal. He was sure that Nora had done this on purpose, served it early and not in the dining room. She got up and served a plate and set it down in front of him across the table from Jean. She said, "It was a small thing, wasn't it?"

Maintaining the fiction between them he said, "Yes, pretty small," and disposed of the matter with a question to Jean about her ballet lesson. Her answer that it had gone well was what he expected, all he had expected. He regarded her for moment, noting that her long dark hair was in need of attention. A last bite or two and, excusing herself, Jean got up from the table and left the room.

"I like this fish," Hugh said, to break the silence. Nora was now puttering at the sink and when she answered it had nothing to do with the fish.

"My guess is, you went to see your priest, didn't you?"

"Is that what you think whenever I go out?"

"Didn't you?" She still had her back turned to him.

He said, "In the first place he's not 'my priest' anymore. But I still feel kindly toward him, as a person. Why shouldn't I, we were sort of friends. He's making trouble for himself and I thought I'd give him a little free advice."

"What did he give you? Forgiveness for your sins, maybe?"

"Baloney!" Hugh said and went at his food.

He thought that at least for tonight this would be the end of the matter. For quite some time, in the den, they talked about the afternoon's event, though it was he almost entirely who did the talking. "I think it's a lie," he said, "but he's making it work. So far, anyway. It's scary. Those two fires. And why old Stark's church when he's more like them, in a way, than the rest of us are? Maybe it wasn't blacks that did that one."

Nora barely looked up from her magazine to say, "Well, we have it coming."

"Maybe so. But it's not likely to right anything. Just fuel to the fire. What a time!"

When he finally stopped talking he noticed that Nora was gazing straight ahead at the wall as though entranced by something there. She suddenly said, "There's a new psychiatrist in town. In the old Decherd building." She was still gazing at the wall.

"Oh," Hugh said. "Well, we've got plenty of use for him here." A moment's reflection called up his vexation again. "Or do you mean, 'I've' got use for him? To cure me of the priest."

"It might help."

Still more vexed, he said, "Do you think maybe I'm homosexual, and we're lovers?"

"No. Though that's crossed my mind. At times."

"You mean, my 'performance.' Look. And I've told you this a dozen times. I do have a little sentimental guilt, a sort of nostalgia . . . which is getting less and less. I assure you, that's 'all.' And by the way, I think you're the one who needs a psychiatrist. You've gotten to be a real fanatic on the subject. I see it in your eyes every time poor Father Riley even gets mentioned. It's crazy. And also by the way, I wish you'd look at me instead of that wall."

She did, straight-on, with that look his words had conjured, like eyes with a core too burning hot for their darkness to wholly obscure. This lasted but an instant. She said, "Crazy? I know you better than you know yourself . . . And maybe your priest, too."

"What does that mean?"

She stood up. "I'm going up to bed."

He let her go without comment and sat for another hour doggedly browsing through magazines. When he finally went up he found her either asleep or pretending to be. In the bed beside her he came hesitantly to a decision. He put his hand on her hip and left it there for a time. There was no response.

In the night he had a dream that came, as it were, in defiance of his will. At his bathroom window he looked out and saw spread out down there the little village of Loretta, with a few old cars parked in the square and people, many in overalls, walking about or conversing or seated on benches on the lawn of the old stained-brick courthouse. He seemed to recognize most of them, but before he could be sure, the scene shifted. It was the chapel, drawing nearer, all at once revealing its interior where he, with his mother and father and Wilbur, was seated in a front pew. There at the altar decrepit Father Kennedy was saying, muttering the Mass, while he, Hugh, as his habit was, held his gaze turned upward to the window on his right. For there was Christ in midair, a wonder, ascending with lordly outstretched arms to the blue of heaven above. As He passed from sight Hugh opened his eyes to the darkness of his bedroom.

8

Except occasionally in court or on the streets and always at a distance as great as he could manage, Wilbur had not seen either his former wife or Hugh since the divorce. The one small break in the mutual silence was that occasion when Jean, with obvious reluctance, had come to his office to thank him for the birthday presents he had sent—the tutu and tights and slippers that he could ill afford. Hugh's work, surely. An olive branch? If so, it was cause for regret that he, Wilbur, had sent the presents at all. He wanted nothing from Hugh, nothing to mediate the bitterness he lived with night and day. No, "hatred" was the fitting description, a hatred eating away at his guts, a cancer that he valued too much to even desire its removal. Sometimes in more thoughtful moments he was able to recognize that this, or mainly this, was the reason he did not pick up and leave this seething town.

Wilbur had more time than he needed to think about the matter. He, with his family, had arrived in Lakepoint a year and a half ago, as a virtual stranger now. But he had high hopes and immediately leased a small office in the Dandridge Building a block off the square. Here he had established his law practice, expecting, without solid reason, that it would prosper. He had not foreseen the extent of the competition, especially that of his brother, who was also city attorney. Instead of the well-to-do with such as contract problems, what came to him were the dregs: small victims of their own folly, unlucky or reckless entrepreneurs, penniless felons he had to defend by court appointment. The result was a scanty uncertain living that had never improved by much. And such relief as had finally come was because he was single now.

Truly it was not much. The freedom gained was time on his hands that he mostly spent in brooding. That drawn-out trial in all its ugliness, like a reel that would not wear out, kept running, running through his mind. With highlights here and there, like the sight of Nora's furious twisted face. Lying bitch! How had she managed through the years of their marriage to keep her true self hidden? The hints had been there, plain in retrospect, glimmering in her eyes sometimes. And he in his innocence standing by while she turned their daughter against him. Just here was the cruelest cut, made plain despite his willful blindness in the judge's chambers that day. The mother's day of triumph, the daughter swallowed up.

That day (more than a year gone by?) was the last time he had been in his daughter's presence. From a distance, always with a jump of his pulse, he had seen her now and then, accompanied by her mother. But one day she was alone. His office was on the second floor with a window that looked out over Payne Street just in sight of the square. Often, when Miss Miller, his part-time secretary was not present, he stood at that window, looking down, gazing off into the square, searching maybe for a glimpse of Jean. And finally there she was, turning into Payne Street, walking unaccompanied. He thought that his heart really did stop, that she was coming here, coming to visit him. He was wrong. All but smitten he watched her pass by, no upward glance, walking with her dancer's grace but not quite with a look of assurance. He watched her out of sight. Going where? At last he turned and with empty eyes stood in front of a file cabinet where, he seemed to remember, there was something that needed his attention.

This event, it seemed to him the next day, had been a sort of harbinger, a preparation soon to be fulfilled. It was this feeling that caused him, when someone knocked, almost to leap out of his chair. But the knock was too demanding, and so, as he approached the door, he did not expect a surprise. He was more than surprised, however. It was Cap Waters.

For a long time now, as it had come to be, Wilbur had viewed the increasing disorders of the town with cool detachment, a spectator's eye. He had witnessed and vaguely enjoyed Cap Waters's performance, like a good show, in front of the courthouse. But here, confronted with the man in person, Wilbur had the unwelcome feeling that he was about to be sucked in.

It was a notion made more forceful by the thought of what he had overheard only this morning at the courthouse, as though that talk was somehow the cause that led to Waters's coming here. It was about the Quals boy, rumors (so many rumors these days) that he had turned up in Wharton City where he had kin: that he had been sighted, one version said, while another said that he had been captured by the police and would soon be returned to Lakepoint. So it went and, vaguely like a consequence, here was Cap Waters at Wilbur's door.

Before Wilbur could speak, the bass voice said, "They tell me you the one for this."

For what? Wilbur almost said, and only by gesture invited him in.

The man seemed too big for this small room and certainly for the imperilled chair on which he had straightway seated himself. Wilbur, at the secretary's desk, eyed him: the face, large-boned and kettle-black, the wide-set eyes that for one slack moment glanced about as if they did not think much of what they saw. "Goan try you, now," Waters said. "Them others ain't got the guts. Lib'rals, yeah. Your brother one of them." He might not have meant his direct gaze to be intimidating.

"Well?" Wilbur finally said.

"Some white som'bitch taken a shot at me."

In Waters's pause, Wilbur decided not to recommend the police. "Did you get a look at him?"

"Naw. Waiting in a car. Right where you go in our part of town. Had me in the headlights." Then, "That ain't why I come here, though."

"All right," Wilbur said.

Looking hard at Wilbur's face, he said, "I want you to start me a lawsuit. On the mayor and the whole goddamn bunch of them."

Wilbur hesitated. "You've got to have grounds."

"Yeah, grounds. I got grounds. That whole nigger-killing police force they won't do nothing about. Want a new one, with blacks on it and a black chief."

"Aren't there already some on it? One, anyway."

"Yeah, a 'Tom.' Ain't worth a shit. Just go along licking white people's ass." Then, a clear challenge, "Will you do it?"

Wilbur looked away from him, casting about in his mind, in the waiting silence that barely admitted the wail of a distant siren. He said, "The only chance you'd have in court would be to prove something on them. I mean evidence of . . ."

"Got evidence. A eyewitness . . . of them killing that boy."

"Yes, I saw her. But . . ." He paused. "Look. You haven't got a dead body to show. And that boy could still turn up; it hasn't been that long."

"He ain't going to turn up. 'Less they find him floating in that lake."

"It would have to be something like that. And by the way, I guess you've heard the rumors."

"I heard them. Heard them this morning. Damn lies. White shit all over them." To Wilbur's relief he stood up, the bulk of him filling the room. But he paused. The wide black eyes now trained on Wilbur's face held a dangerous light . . . hard to withstand. "You same as the rest of them. Ain't a white man in this town to trust. 'Cept maybe that little old priest. And he come from way off someplace." He turned and went out, slamming the door hard enough to endanger the frosted glass.

Wilbur got up and stepped to the window. Waters, on the street below, walked to where his car was parked, illegally, and drove away. He was not a liar, Wilbur thought; he believed in what he said. And what would he do now, with all that dammed-up rage inside him?

But something caught Wilbur's gaze, seized upon it. He all but held his breath as she approached, hatless in the sun, walking, it seemed, with a tentative look. To his door? Across the street from his building she stopped. She seemed to look up toward his window, but there was no telling whether she saw him. Then she was crossing the street.

Should he be seated or standing? He was still standing when he heard her footsteps. Then, ever so lightly, her knock three times on the glass. He heard himself say, "Come in."

The door slowly opened and there she was, in a plain brown cotton dress and, as her mother's never had been, her dark hair in need of combing. She seemed taller than he remembered. He said, "I'm glad to see you."

She had not taken her hand off the doorknob. Her lips hung open for a moment before she quietly said, "I came to thank you for the presents."

"I'm glad you did. Please come sit down."

She hesitated. "I have to go to . . ."

"Please."

Uncertainly she took her hand from the knob and stepped to the nearest chair against the wall. There she sat upright, knees together, hands clasped on her lap. She said, "Just for a minute. I have to go to my lesson."

"I hope you'll stay long enough to tell me about yourself. What you've been doing. About your dancing."

"Oh I go twice a week. My teacher says I'm getting better and better."

"I knew you would. You were wonderful even back when I used to see you." This made her lower her gaze, look down at the floor. He quickly said, "What else do you do? Do you have some friends? A boy friend?"

She hesitated. "I did, sort of. But . . ." She stopped; nothing followed. Suddenly Wilbur felt that he could finish it for her. He hesitated. But an impulse made him say, rashly, "Your mother broke it up?"

Her glance was only half a denial. "He was a Catholic. I hate Catholics." She blinked, uneasy.

Wilbur mulled it for a second or two. He said, "I used to be one."

With eyes a little wider, a flash of brightness across them, she said, "They've got that awful priest."

Father Riley, Wilbur thought. He had seen him there with Cap Waters in front of the courthouse. "Old Rock Head." It was something he had heard children shout one day when the priest was walking by.

"Why 'awful'?"

Jean looked evasive. "He does bad things," she murmured.

"Can you tell me what bad things?"

Again she hesitated. In a voice almost a whisper, she said, "To little children." A moment later, with a faintly urgent lift of her voice, "They're all talking about it."

"All?"

She shook her head determinedly.

Wilbur was silent for a moment, considering another question, when suddenly Jean stood up. "I have to go to my lesson now."

"Please don't hurry."

"I have to." Then, "Thank you," she said and turned to leave.

"Just a second, please," Wilbur said, and when she stopped, looked back at him, he said, "I hope you came because you wanted to. And nobody sent you."

"I wanted to," she said. "Nobody sent me." Then she was out through the open door before he could decently tell her goodbye.

From his window Wilbur followed her progress, hurried now, up the street and out of sight. Sixteen and still a child, he thought ... the work of her mother's hands. And he, as helpless as he had always been, sentenced to watch from a distance. From a window, he thought, as now, like a spy on the turbulent world. With a mental shrug he turned away, inviting other thoughts. The priest came back. Only talk, idle or vicious talk? But he had heard, read in newspapers, recent stories about such things. It was not his business. Nothing was his business.

He had a case, a petty thief up for trial in an hour. He was on hand, arguing what he knew to be a futile defense. Afterward he had supper at the usual café and until night set in walked along the lake front. Something briefly disturbed his sleep that night, but he did not know until next day that a building had been set afire and also that a police officer had been killed.

9

THAT NEXT DAY Cap Waters was picked up at his home and brought to the police station for questioning. The killing of the policeman, who in trying to catch the arsonist got his skull broken, had already produced a climate that would have shaken other men in Waters's shoes. He, however, in the face of a small but threatening crowd held under restraint ten steps away, got right out of the police car as though he had come here with nothing special in mind. Inside, confronted by Chief Bostick and flanked by another policeman and a detective, he retained much the same demeanor through an interview that included some harsh accusations. Even these made little more difference than a tightening of his jaw, and no discernable change in his voice. He knew nothing about the matter, not till this morning; had spent his evening with a friend; had put nobody up to anything. They gave up and drove him home, dismissing him with the accustomed solemn admonishments.

Waters supposed that with a little research around the community he might discover the culprit. But what had happened was nothing more than payback, and his mind was busy elsewhere.

He was not worried about possible truth in the rumors. The boy was dead somewhere, no doubt in the lake, and all that talk he had heard about for the last day or two was nothing but Whitey still hoping, whistling in the dark. That kind of talk was a snag, though, holding things back. What he needed (which he knew well enough before that pissant lawyer said it) was the boy's body to shut them up. After a couple of days a dead body would come to the top and keep floating for quite a while. But it already had been quite a while and a good deal more besides. But if the body had floated in to shore it might be there yet, tangled in reeds and brush that made it hard to see. He could still hope for that. Anyhow rumors like those he'd heard would wear out pretty soon; he could bide his time. And last night's doings, whatever else could be said about them, were hard at work already to keep the pressure up.

But along in the night of the next day, Waters was all of a sudden stricken by the worst of news. At the time he was in his house drawing up another public announcement, alone because his wife had gone back to live in Atlanta. The knock at his door was surely quiet, but he would not remember it so. An opening shot, a signal, was how he would recall it, seeing himself jolted onto his feet, hurrying, his hand seizing the doorknob. But he remembered, exactly as they were, the words spoken by the man across the threshold from him, whispered words, like the devil's voice secretly uttered close beside his ear. "Eddie Quals done come back."

Waters understood; it was just that he could not focus at first, that he needed time to compel his scattered thoughts. Finally, "You seen him? With your own eyes?"

"Sho have. He down there at his mama's house."

"How long?" Waters said, all he could manage so far.

"How long he been there? . . . Since a little while after dark."

"All right." In a single flash his clarity came back. "Go tell him come up here. And not talk to nobody else. Right now!"

"Okay. But he liable not want to come."

"You tell him I said come up here. And do it quick."

In the interval Waters did not sit down or even move more than a step or two out of his tracks. His gaze was trained on the wall where there was a picture: himself in the embrace of a black civil rights leader named Amid. But this was not what he was seeing. He was envisioning the white faces, gloating, looking back at him. Fool nigger, in his own trap, one only a nigger would hit on. That was the talk, or would be . . . No way to answer back.

He was still standing there with the blood gone hot in his face, when he heard the footsteps on his porch. Three quick strides and he snatched the door open. "Get in here, boy." Then, "Not you, Link, get on away from here," and he slammed the door against him.

Quals, a slim, light-colored boy, stood there looking sheepish but somehow defiant too. "What you want with me? I ain't done nothing but get scared and run away."

Waters stood glaring down at him, his hands clenching. "And then you come back here. Messed up everything. How many people seen you?"

"What I messed up?"

"How many people seen you since you got back?"

"Mama. Link. One or two more. I turn myself in, they ain't gonna do nothing much to me. What Mama say." That glare was making him more and more uneasy.

"You going back, boy. Going to drive you to Atlanta, put you on a bus going a long way from here. And you ain't coming back. I'll give you some money."

Quals looked away from him, glanced at the door. "I don't want to. What I going do someplace way off?" What he felt was more than uneasiness now. "I got to . . ."

"Don't mess with me, boy." The words "fool nigger" flashed across his mind. True words. "Let's get going." He lifted a hand, a fist, and gestured toward the door.

"I told Mama . . ."

"I said 'Get going!'"

Quals retreated half a step, white-eyed, wetting his lips. "Mama say come right back."

In a flash of movement Waters seized his arm, swung him around, half dragged him to the door and out. The boy fighting against him now, crying, "Let me loose, let me loose," they reached the car. But Quals dropped suddenly to his knees and with a lurch broke free of the grip on his arm. He was free for a mere second, because it was just at this point that Waters in a surge of blind fury did the thing he could afterward remember only as if mirrored through a cloud. He was able to recall what it was like to hit the boy, hit him with all the strength of his powerful right arm, and that somehow the car bumper had been a participant in this moment. Just as clearly he remembered, as at one with the blow itself, the words "fool nigger" raging in his mind. What followed was an interlude of silence everywhere, from which he emerged to find himself on his knees beside the boy. It seemed as if he had known for quite a while that this was a dead boy.

When at last he stood up he was looking around him. Except for a few lighted windows there was nothing to see, and no sound but a dog somewhere. His next act came to him like the first step in a brilliant plan that had somehow invented itself. He opened the back door of the car and, almost without effort, lifted the body and placed it as best he could on the floor behind the front seat. Then he was driving, with cautious speed, still directed by that plan.

All the way, skirting the lighted center of town, nearing, crossing the bridge, the single thought possessing him was that of his destination.

A creek that entered the lake, where brush and water weeds intertwined. But then, as he descended from the bridge, a brief slip of the mind let something in. Fool. Too late, too late. He banished the thought by force and, thinking of the creek mouth, drove on for the little distance to where a dirt lane branched from the pavement.

It was quick work, in moonlight glittering on riffled water, a sheen on the lake beyond. He carried the body, dead boy weighing nothing, and ankle-deep in muck at the water's edge, submerged it in the tangle of weeds and branches. Slogging out, on firm ground once more, he hurried as if in headlong retreat from words that followed behind him.

It was this urgency that caused him, as he came out onto the pavement, almost to crash dead-center into a swerving car. He left it standing motionless there behind him, already thinking, Go where? Home? Then he thought, Atlanta! freed from all pursuit. This was his decision. Passing carefully through town and onto Highway 10, he set out for Atlanta a hundred miles away.

He did not go far. Driving slower and slower, he finally turned around. He passed through town again and into the district where not a soul and only one lighted window were to be seen . . . But morning would come.

Nevertheless he drove on to his house and parked and went in. The lights were still burning. He washed his face and hands, forgetful of his shoes. He sat down and gazed at the wall where the picture was, the embrace. It was not that he owed anything to white man's justice. Black faces came to mind, accusing, unbearable. He would leave everything to Ruby Quals . . . his house, everything. Then, what more?

He sat there into the deep of night. Finally he got up and wrote on a piece of paper addressed to Ruby Quals and left it on the table by the door. Then he turned off the lights and left.

It was not yet daylight when he parked his car, trying to think what had guided him here. He was in the lot next to one other car, beside the chapel, and back behind it, dimly figured in the night, was the little building where the priest must live. Not pausing to think what was in his mind, he passed through the gate and on to the dark doorway. Even his knock was indiscrete, much too loud. It brought a quick result. A light came on and then the priest stood there in silhouette. An empty moment passed.

"What is it?"

"It's me. Cap Waters."

Father Riley did hesitate, but not for long. "Come in, Mr. Waters."

Inside in the dim light of a table lamp they stood regarding each other in silence. It came to Waters suddenly that "Father" was what they called him. So small a man, half the size of himself. Father Riley said, "Would you like to sit down?"

One chair and a threadbare sofa were the choices, and trusting it would not break he chose the chair. To no purpose his shifting gaze took in the bareness of the room: nothing but holy pictures for relief.

"You must have something to tell me," Father Riley said. From the sofa where he sat with folded hands he was studying Waters's face.

Now? Out with it? Why had he come? But he had come. In a too-loud voice he said, "I kilt that boy."

His words seemed to register slowly, knitting Father Riley's brow. "I don't understand."

"I never went to. Only just to hit him. 'Cause he come back, messed up everything. Made a damn fool nigger out of me." He fell silent. His gaze drifted away.

At last Father Riley said, "The Quals boy, you mean. And he's dead?"

Waters looked as if he was dreaming. It was a long while before he said, "Been thinking how you warned me. Told me Wait. I wouldn't hear. Wanted it too bad. To shame them, make them do right."

This seemed to be all that Waters meant to say. He did not move or look at Father Riley, and the deepening silence at length made clear the threadlike whine of some insect. Finally, "What do you plan to do?" Father Riley said.

Waters still did not look at him. His voice deep as a growl, he said, "I don't know. 'Cept leave out."

"You're bound by law to turn yourself in, you know. It was an accident."

"No way. White man's law ain't nothing to me. No way."

"It's God's law too."

"Yeah. Might be, somewheres else. Might be I'll find out where it's at and go live there." He got to his feet, towering in the room. "You can go tell them about me. Keep yourself out of trouble. I'm on my way out right now."

"Wait," Father Riley said. He was standing now. "Why did you come to me?"

Waters hesitated. "I don't know, I just come. I'm leaving now."

"Can I give you my blessing? I don't know anything else I can do for you."

"That be fine."

Father Riley moved closer and lifted his hand. Waters, understanding, bent down a little to receive it on his forehead. Then he turned and went to the door.

"One more thing," Father Riley said.

With his hand on the knob, Waters paused.

"Where is the boy?"

A moment's stillness and Waters said, "Other side the lake . . . 'bout a mile from the bridge where a creek run in." Then he went out into first dawn light.

10

FATHER RILEY, after an interval of meditation and with some reluctance, did what the law required of him. Still in early daylight he drove through town, through the all-but-deserted square, to the police station and reported the matter in full to the sergeant on duty. Within hours the news was all over town, news that to most of the white majority was soon made the more toothsome by the recovery of the boy's body. It was midafternoon when Nora, from the busy mouth of her hairdresser, heard about it. To her, at first, it was not good news: she had hoped with some passion for Waters's success. But this was before she understood just how the priest was involved. This put the hint of a smile on her lips. Friend and confidant to the killer, the town's black nemesis. A gift from heaven, was her ironical thought.

Driving home and then at her dressing table in front of the mirror, her satisfaction kept increasing. Together with the rumors on all those busy tongues, with even children's mockery, was not this brew quite strong enough to execute her purpose? At least in time it would be.

In time? she thought. Soon, very soon, would be much more to her liking. And as for "her rumors," she told herself, they might well be the truth. Had she not seen that little girl (McDougal was her name) kneeling in rapture at his feet, her hand in his, all open to priestly snares concealed in pious words. Snares. That was how they worked, priests and other fathers too, ensnaring the minds and hearts of children helpless to resist. Just as it was with Father Riley, so it had been with her own. Garbage. Her own Jehovah perched in his high-back chair, descanting upon the glories of a nonexistent world, bearing a leather belt for thunder. She reviewed the years it had taken, a passage waveringly slow, to break from his dominion. But at last the break was complete, for she had been strong enough. That hatred too was necessary had never blunted her purpose. All justified: no devil, Satan, or Lucifer to pursue her ever again. Lucifer, she thought, recalling a certain moment years ago. It was when in a textbook she had discovered the derivation of the word. "Bearer of light." That was a luminous moment. For the first time in a long, long while, she thought of "him" again.

Nora's image in the mirror was especially pleasing to her just now: her hair cut a little shorter, swept above her ears, a bluish tint that palely relieved its darkness. A touch of lipstick made her mouth more vivid, a complement to these moments of new brightness in her eyes. Forbidden vanity, she thought, and smiled into the mirror. But something happened to the smile, a blurring that deeply shadowed her whole face, so that an altered image peered from out of a darkness at her. An instant only. It was but a trick of the light, a cloud passing quickly across the slanted rays of the sun. She was not superstitious. A moment more and that altered image had quite gone out of her mind.

But a real interruption soon followed, Jean standing at her door. "I'm back, Mama," she said. Then, "You look nice. Your hair."

"Thank you, dear." Something she had been mulling leaped into her mind. She made her decision and said, "We haven't really talked in the last few days. I was just wondering. Have you heard any more . . . about the priest?"

"I have about him and the black man. Waters. Everybody has."

"No. I mean the other thing."

As always in this matter Jean's face assumed an expression of faint alarm, a sort of conspiratorial look. "They're still talking about it. A lot of them are. Girls, anyway. I think grown people, too." She waited, with an air of wanting to please.

"I've heard something," Nora said. "They say it's the McDougal girl . . . for one. She's in his instruction class. I saw her once, when I went there with Hugh. The two of them. They didn't know I saw. He had his hands on her."

That expression of alarm, intensified, was plain in Jean's face now.

"Do you know her?" Nora said.

Jean looked away, looked back. "I know her big sister, I think . . . a little."

"All right," Nora said. "It's just that we need to know. It's important. Very important. Just keep your ears open. And pry a little. Find out what you can."

"I will, Mama. I promise."

"Good." To make an end of it, Nora turned away. Then she remembered. "Wait. Don't forget what I told you about Hugh. Don't breath even a word of it to him."

"I won't, Mama."

When Hugh came in an hour later it was not Nora who broached the subject of the day's excitement. This was her new strategy in these days, simply to wait, assuming an air of disengagement from matters in which she might stumble. She did not have long to wait, long enough only for Hugh to fix drinks and bring them into the den. "I guess you know what happened today," he said and sat down in the chair across from hers.

"Yes. I heard all about it at my hairdresser's. Where I hear everything." She sipped from her drink.

"A hell of a thing. The fool should have known better, right in the face of the odds against him. Now he's cut his own throat."

"It's a shame. I know how he must have felt, though . . . how they all feel. I'm sure he didn't mean to kill the boy." She took another sip. She was waiting.

"Well, so be it."

In the interval of silence she guardedly watched his lips, waiting.

"I like your hair."

"Thank you."

Hugh drew a breath, drank, and then said, "Poor Father Riley, too. . . . Forgive me for bringing him up," he dryly added.

"All right." Then, not too quickly, "What about him?"

"This just sets him up more. Waters's pet crony. It's not like he didn't have troubles already. Those rumors. This town's gone crazy with rumors. You must have heard them, or about them. They're calling him a child molester."

Studiedly Nora said, "I have heard something about it." She caught herself and added, "Mostly just today, at my hairdresser's." A little slip, perhaps, but Hugh's face registered nothing.

"If I didn't mention it," he said, "it's because of your attitude. The whole thing's groundless gossip. Ridiculous. He's incapable of a thing like that."

She gave a nod, a little ambivalent, maybe. If so, again he did not notice.

"At least I tried to warn him about Waters. He wouldn't listen. He'd better be listening now." Hugh was quiet for a moment, lifted his glass. "I wonder what kind of a son-of-a-bitch started these lies?"

Trying to make her face look blank, she considered things she might say. "I can't imagine." "Stories in the news." She rejected each one and said nothing, settling for an unambivalent nod.

But a curious thing was beginning to happen, something in her head that was like a thought but was not a thought exactly ... something slowly blossoming.

"I'd forgot," Hugh suddenly said. "We'd better get going, we're going to be late."

That would be fine, she thought. So would everything be fine. It was as if, just by a little, she had had too much to drink and found herself, alone with gladness, at a distance from this world. Alone, it seemed, but not alone, for Jean would be at her side.

"Let's get going," Hugh said and got to his feet.

She did as expected and went into the hall and took her purse from the hanger.

Those curious moments did not last long but something from them stuck with her. She noticed it at the party, observing details, gesturings of heads and hands, teeth exposed in drunken laughter. And familiar voices that came across as not so familiar now. There was talk of Waters and of the priest, to which she listened intently, savoring it all. Like a stranger, was how she felt. Did they notice? She could see no indication there.

The next morning it seemed to Nora that she was quite herself again. But this was only at first: something was different. And through her experience of that day, in which she closely observed herself, she began to feel that this residual difference might prove to be a lasting thing. It amounted to pleasure, almost a delight, born of her secret knowledge that she alone, her very hand, had brought all this to be. So it was that from this day she went her rounds like a spy. Best of all was her hairdresser's shop, but there were other places. She sought out those where people gathered, and she lingered on to listen. To listen and, when the moment was right, to inject a few studied words.

II

In the torrid August heat outside the municipal building, Father Riley made one more in the slow-moving line of voters. Because of the heat, it was a little something to be thankful for that the man behind him steadfastly kept an emphatic distance between them. As if a leper stood in their midst, Father Riley thought. So it had come to be in the course of these last two weeks, in which no denial on his part or on that of friends had seemed to make an impression.

The rumors, as it first appeared, were so obviously groundless that he had all but dismissed them as certain to be short-lived. Soon, though, more than ever, he began to notice how many heads turned to watch him pass by in the streets. Then it was a coolness of clerks in the stores and the silence that greeted him in the Lakeside Café where he sometimes ate his meals. One of his parishioners, Thomas Bollen, finally drove it home to him. "'Course we know it's all lies," the old man said. He had a shaky high-pitched voice. "But those folks out there, they're not like us Catholics. They don't think much of us just in general."

With an unaccustomed flash of anger Father Riley said, "But what have they got for evidence?"

"Nothing, I figure. Some say it was stories in the newspaper. About bad priests doing such. Messing with little children … It's hurting, though."

Father Riley thought of the children he taught, and played with sometimes in the fenced-in yard behind the church. A moment of revulsion seized him. "No mention of any of my children, that I teach?"

"Not to my knowing. It's just the way they are."

This was bad enough, but there was worse to come, much worse. Soon it was his parishioners who had become the real center of his distress. He had noticed first at a Sunday Mass something new in the faces, hesitant and fleeting looks. It had been little different afterward in the brief social hour, at which, as he also noticed, certain faithful members failed to appear. That was the beginning and it grew worse. Daily Masses, always poorly attended, drew still fewer people, and on the second Sunday he was looking at a congregation diminished by nearly a third. It was then, departing from his regular homily, that he made his first public denial of the rumors. He told them that this, abuse of children, was perhaps of all the mortal sins the one most abhorrent to him. In conclusion he spoke of gossip, in itself a most serious sin, like murder in fact by reason of its potential to destroy. But afterward he could not be sure as to how his words were received. Though some took pains to approach him and express their outrage also, he knew that there should have been more.

He set out on a small campaign that, as he soon concluded, was ill advised. It was to visit certain families in their homes: social calls during which, incidentally, he would drop some earnest words of reassurance. He completed two such calls with what he felt was only ambiguous success (their faces were hard to read) and moved on with diminished confidence to another. This was to be the last one. It was the home of Mrs. McDougal, a widow whose younger daughter was in his classes. He mounted onto the shaded porch and knocked. He waited and, hearing music inside, knocked louder. Still he waited. Her car was in the driveway. He started to knock again and did not. He turned away and pausing beside his car thought he saw, just for an instant, a face at the window.

A mistake, he thought, driving away, ruefully chiding himself. In such a case, insistence clearly was not the chord to strike. From this moment on, he promised himself, his defense would be confident silence. Silence and also prayer, of course, Christ's warranty to all.

This was the frame of mind in which he decided against his newly adopted behavior: this hiding, as it were, from the public eye. He would go about, as always ... to his regular café for a meal, to the usual stores, careful only not to do so for the sake of mere defiance. And it so happened that the very next day gave him, though he had almost forgot, a special reason to go forth. Along in the afternoon, on foot, he set out for the municipal building where he was scheduled to vote.

He ignored the attention his presence drew and pretended not even to hear remarks designed to be overheard. An hour of this in the blazing sun and at last, inside the building, he received along with his ballot the scrutiny of official eyes. He marked it cooly, after thought, as though it truly mattered, choosing Baker the Chevrolet man as the one perhaps the more harmless.

He exited the building into the parking lot. There, lounging among motorcycles parked close together, was a small group of teenage boys... in black skullcaps and identical flowing shirts. All in the very same instant, it seemed, their eyes had fastened on him. In silence they followed as he walked past, and it was not until he had got almost to the street that he heard a voice. "Where you going, Rock Head?" And another, "Kiddies waiting for you?" A third said, "Need a escort?" He went on, careful not to change his pace.

He had got past the long block where cars were parked and turned into the nearly empty street before he heard it, what he had been listening for: a distant revving of motors. He kept to his pace, hearing them, the sound of the motors louder. Then, like thunder, they rounded the corner behind him, two up on the sidewalk overtaking him now. At his heels and also beside him, they kept to his pace, revving their motors to a pitch that half drowned the razzing voices. There was one he clearly heard: "Good stuff waiting for you?" He went on, his eyes fixed straight ahead.

Then a crossing, an open street ahead. He did not pause, stepped out, and found himself encircled, around and around him, the circle tightening, thundering in his ears. Something, a handlebar, grazed his arm. It happened again but harder, a blow this time that forced him to a halt. Around and around, the jeering faces. Ugly, satanic, he thought. He stood there, standing straight.

But there was a break, a car horn, two cars forcing their way. The circle split. He passed through at his regular pace, with eyes fixed straight ahead. He was not pursued any farther.

Especially in light of all that had preceded, this was much more than a stupid prank of roughneck boys. How to deal with it all? Over and over, and still more urgently today, he turned the question in his mind. Evening Mass, with three worshipers only, interrupted, but the question dogged him on into the night. At length he fastened on a thought, a hesitant one requiring consideration. It was to phone, or maybe visit, Bishop Wells in Atlanta. The thought did not please him; he was no mere novice unfit to deal with troubles that were his own. He would not do it ... or maybe he would. The question was still there unresolved when he fell asleep at last.

Because of a single interlude his night was a harrowing one. As he recalled the next morning, he had spent part of it conversing in a dream that he knew to be a dream only because there was no other practical explanation. In truth the episode mostly lacked a beginning and an end, but the essence, the extended middle, took place in all the stark illumination of a lightning strike. There was a knock, and opening the door he instantly discerned, to his astonishment, that it was Bishop Wells. There was something by way of explanation: on a trip and passing through town, the bishop had heard of Father Riley's troubles and decided to call. There was an apology for the hour. Next, in the unmitigated light of the lamp that Father Riley had turned on, they were seated, he on the chair opposite Bishop Wells on the sofa. Although he had never before seen the bishop in person, he was more than surprised. He was looking at a small man with a wizened face whose inconstant too-large bloodshot eyes might have belonged to another. The baggy threadbare clerical garb, as if it had been handed down to him by his predecessor, was equally surprising. But the bishop's voice was precise, authoritative, a fact that at the start comforted Father Riley. The bishop said, "Such things, and worse things, happen more often than you think. Much more. And increasingly."

"I'm sorry to hear it," Father Riley murmured.

"It's the world. It's everywhere, this and other evils. You can see it yourself, can't you, Father? right here in your own small parish."

"In the town, at least," Father Riley said.

"Everywhere. In your parish too. Breaking away, faith departed. Yet you have done nothing wrong."

"But it may be, Your Grace, that I did not ..."

"No use to defend them. The decay, the rot, is universal ... in high places as well as low." His changeful eyes looked up at the ceiling. "You, they all, call me 'Your Grace,' but look at me. Do you see grace in my countenance, in my attire? Do you?"

Suddenly appalled, Father Riley could only stare at him.

"No. My heritage is gone. God has withdrawn his grace. He has left us subject to a new regime." He paused, the inconstant eyes shut for a moment. "No," he said. "Not new. Old, as old as the world. The apostle John was mistaken. The Ancient Prince, after all, never was cast out. Can you not see that?"

Father Riley was barely able to shake his head in denial.

"No. Yet you have done nothing. Nothing wrong and nothing in your ministry. Indeed, 'nothing' is the word. Our Word."

As if a freeze had taken hold, Father Riley waited.

"Your one mistake was a great one. Your choice of a profession. Cast it off. Or see yourself burnt alive in the blast of their evil tongues."

The stillness was more than a stillness. It was a place where time itself was stilled eternally.

"I am on my way," the bishop said, rising to his feet. "I regret that I have no blessing to bestow. Goodbye."

Then he was gone, leaving Father Riley alone in the stark unquenchable light.

12

Nora and Jean had just got through cleaning up the breakfast dishes when the telephone rang. For a moment after Nora had picked up the receiver and said hello, there was only silence on the line. Then a voice, feeble sounding but clear enough, said, "This is Ellen McDougal." It was Nora's time to pause, but then she said, "Yes," and stood listening in a sort of vague alarm to the woman's words. When they stopped, Nora said, "You mean, right now?" and finally, with more confidence, "That will be all right." She was looking at Jean when she put the phone down.

"That was Mrs. McDougal. She's coming to talk with me. You must have mentioned it to someone, what I told you. Along with my name."

Jean's face, blank at first, took on a stricken look. "You didn't tell me not to, Mama. Except just to Hugh."

"I'm sure I did. I didn't want my name connected with it. At least until there was more to go on, from somewhere else, if at all. Well, I can handle it." But how? she thought.

"I'm awful sorry, Mama." Her face continued to show it. "I just didn't remember."

How? It was out of that expression of heartfelt sorrow on Jean's face that an idea, halting at first, took shape in Nora's mind. Too much, too bold? Finally she said, "Have you heard anything more . . . girls talking, maybe?"

Jean thought for a moment, straining, as it seemed. "I can't think of anything."

"Try." Nora waited, watching Jean's face, her confidence growing now. "Something you'd almost forgotten? Like, maybe, one of them saying she knew somebody who really saw it . . . saw it happening?"

It was puzzlement now that clouded Jean's face. She finally said, "But who?"

"You might not even have known their names. Just girls you know by sight." Nora paused, hesitant, but inspiration seized her. "This is a terrible thing, Jean. Worse than you know. Little children never recover, really recover, from this kind of thing. And it's happening right down there at that Catholic church. I know because I saw, could tell what it meant. And it happens so often among them. That dirty man must be got rid of. No matter what we have to do . . . Do you understand?"

In the lingering stillness the puzzled expression died slowly out of her face. But it was a while yet before she said, "I understand, Mama. I think I do."

"Good."

She sat in the den alone, waiting. That moment of alarm on the telephone was almost past remembering now. A coolness, a sense of mastery, had taken hold to stay, as if all uncertain things lay waiting for the sure touch of her hand. The doorbell rang. A few quick steps and she was there, inviting into her home a small and most unformidable and shaken little woman. In a plain rumpled cotton dress, auburn hair with tufts of gray, a long sad face whose pallor could not have been natural to her. "In here," Nora said, conducting her into the den and to a chair in front of which Mrs. McDougal stood in hesitation.

"Please sit down," Nora said, taking the chair opposite to her, and adding, "I know it's hard for you."

Seated but still hesitant, her gaze unsteady on Nora's face, she finally murmured, "Would you tell me what you saw? My little Polly just cries, says different things. It doesn't sound like the truth."

Pausing to get it right, her voice carefully hushed, Nora said, "All right. I was at the door, looking in. I was there with my husband, because he wanted to walk him back to the church. From the clinic, you know, where the trouble was. He was a little hurt, the priest was. Except for me they all went in his house out back. I finally got tired of waiting and went to the door. At that time nobody was in the room but him and your little girl. They were sitting on the sofa together."

Now the little woman's gaze was steady on Nora's face . . . wide, faintly bloodshot eyes. Almost at a whisper she said, "Please go on."

All at once a new detail seemed needed. Displaying reluctance, Nora said, "I saw him kiss her. On the mouth."

Mrs. McDougal was silent for a moment, her gaze drifting away. "Was there anything more? Did he . . . touch her?"

Nora drew a breath, ending in a sigh. "Yes. He put his hand on her thigh. Just for a moment. I think he heard the others coming back in."

Mrs. McDougal, slowly, as if life itself was draining out of her body, settled back into her chair. She stayed this way for a time, while Nora, alert behind her mask of sympathy, waited. Then, with a small but surprising surge of energy, Mrs. McDougal's voice once more.

"But you should . . . shouldn't you have told me? Or somebody?"

Somehow Nora was not quite prepared for this. It needed study, she was thinking, but swift words leaped to her rescue. "I did. Hugh, my husband. He dismissed it. He said that without more evidence he never would believe it. He used to be one of you, a Catholic. He's still fond of that man. Too fond . . . But you are right, I should have told you. It's worried me all along. In fact, though, I was just about to the point of taking some action."

"What action?"

"Telling about what I saw." She paused. What stood in her mind to say meant taking a risk. But the woman's intent and pallid face was thrust a little forward, waiting. Nora said, "Especially since two days ago when I heard something more."

"Yes?"

"It was my daughter, Jean, who told me." She turned her gaze aside from the waiting face. A risk? She made her decision. "Maybe you had rather hear it from her. She's here, in her room."

"All right," was the faint response.

As though with reluctance, Nora got to her feet and went out.

A few steps on and there on the stairs was Jean, stealthily retreating. "You heard, didn't you?" Nora whispered.

Jean nodded. Her face was pale.

"Come down, dear. Just say what I told you, dear."

"I don't want to, Mama."

"Please. Just for me. It won't take but a minute."

She came, and Nora took her hand and led her.

It was just right, the way Jean stood there mute and shrinking under the weight of Mrs. McDougal's gaze.

"Tell her, dear, what you heard those girls in the park saying. Don't be afraid. Mrs. McDougal wants to know."

Jean's lips parted but her first try was a failure. Then, in a voice pitched higher than her own, she said, "They were talking about somebody who saw it . . . what they were doing."

"You mean the priest. And the little girl," Nora softly said.

A slightly strangled "Yes" was her reply.

There was silence. Mrs. McDougal murmured, "Did they say who?"

Jean shook her head.

"She didn't even know the girls, except to see," Nora said.

"Did you know their names?" Mrs. McDougal said. "Any of them?"

A pause and Jean glanced at her mother. Nora said, "I think you told me one was named Mary something, didn't you? Not much help, though, I'm afraid."

Mrs. McDougal lowered her eyes, looked up again. Maybe you could find them. Ask them."

Jean glanced at her mother again. Quickly Nora said, "We'll try, won't we, dear?"

Jean's nod of affirmation prefaced another silence. Nora said, "You can run along now," and Jean, in that same instant, was gone.

Mrs. McDougal, her face averted, clearly was lost in her thoughts. As if with a plea she looked at Nora again. "I think I'd better go to the bishop. They know how to deal with such things. Don't you think?"

Even when Nora's answer was ready on her tongue she held it back for a space. "I wouldn't," she finally said. "From what I've heard. They take forever. Trying to excuse them. It happens so often, makes a scandal. I've read about cases just recently, in the papers."

Mrs. McDougal pondered. "Maybe I should get a lawyer? Mightn't your husband . . ."

"No. He wouldn't. Because he's fond of the man, if nothing else." The moment was right. She said, "Would you like to know what I would do, without even thinking twice?"

"Please."

"I would go straight to the police. And swear out a warrant against him."

Mrs. McDougal blinked, distressed at the thought. "It seems so... so hard."

"He has it coming, Mrs. McDougal. This is a terrible thing. He has probably done it before, and probably will do again if he's not stopped. Think of all the harm to little children."

At last, "Yes. You are right," she said. "But I must think about it some. Yes." She turned her head, looking around her as if suddenly she had found herself in a different place. She stood up. "Thank you. You are very kind."

Nora saw her to the door, kindly wishing her well, and stood there afterward with a triumphant feeling. Perfect, she thought, recalling how her hand had guided it step by step. She looked around for Jean. She went upstairs to Jean's room and found it empty. She looked and found her nowhere in the house. The fact was a little troubling to her, but after all she knew her daughter.

And this was soon confirmed. A little more than an hour later Jean was back, having merely climbed up to the ridge top, as she often did, for the view. She was quite herself. They went shopping together and stayed out until afternoon.

But throughout these hours and on until evening time Nora, though she kept it well hid, was waiting anxiously. Once she had even made occasion to drive past the police station, and at every stop she was listening for news. The afternoon was long and when, finally, Hugh was at the door, she was up from her chair to greet him.

There was no need for the question she could not ask; he answered it at once. "Have you heard what happened?"

"No. What?" she said, her manner casual.

It was not entirely, or not yet entirely, what she had hoped for: a firm warrant signed, sealed, and delivered to him. The trouble was the police chief, Bostick, who was doubtful about the whole thing, all those rumors. "He's about the only one," Hugh said. "And he won't be there much longer, once they get that crazy election fight settled."

Bostick had tried to put her off, at least until he had had time to go down there and talk to Father Riley. She had agreed to this much, and he had come back with the recommendation that she take it to his superiors, his bishop. But she refused.

"What now?" Nora said, carefully.

"He's to receive it in the morning, the warrant. He'll have to make bail. Of course it's already leaked out. It'll be in the paper tomorrow. And that will be the end of Father Riley, finally . . . one way or the other, in this town." He studied Nora's face for a moment. "I hope you are not gloating."

"Of course not." Was there need to say more? She said, "It's a shame, of course." Then, "But if he's guilty . . ."

"Bunk," Hugh said and headed for the kitchen.

So it was all but accomplished. That Hugh might discover her part in this did not concern her overmuch, for she could handle it. This was what she was thinking upstairs at her dressing table, the while observing in the mirror what seemed, to her pleasure, an odd but somehow enhancing difference in the clear lines of her face.

13

Late in the night, still sleepless, berating himself, Father Riley paced from room to room of his little house. Not only had it been foolish, it had been reckless to the point of scandal that he had not, well before this, taken it to the bishop. Now his urgent calls, three at intervals of half an hour, had got him nothing except that recorded voice: Please leave your message. In any case it was too late now to put a stop to the warrant. Unless . . . Old Chief Bostick had tried, maybe was trying still. (Thank God for him and his trust, a wonder in this town.) And maybe she, poor hysterical woman, would in the course of this long night be brought to a change of mind. Recalling his futile visit to her home, he wondered that this had suggested nothing to him.

But another futile visit, that of only hours ago, was far more persistent in his thoughts. It had occurred to him suddenly that at least he should have a lawyer, and soon afterward, late though it was, he was in his car and on the way.

With only a little trouble he found Hugh's house, where a few lights were burning. He climbed the steps to the porch and knocked. He knocked again and had his hand uplifted for a third try when the porch light came on. The door opened. At once, with a jump of his pulse, he recognized this tall woman in a dressing gown, again recalling from back in his mind that unforgettable first encounter with her. Not instantly but seconds later, an interval in which she appeared more startled than uncertain, he faced that withering look a second time. Before he had quite regained his composure she said, "What is it?"

"Is your husband here?" he managed.

"No." Her eyes steady upon him, she said, "What is it you want?"

There was no right answer, not to her, and he said, "It's a private thing."

"A legal matter?"

He had to nod yes.

"I can guess what it is, Mr. Riley. Hugh knows about it. You are wasting your time. He won't take a case like yours. Not ever." The door came shut in his face, left him standing there with a question in mind that he surely could not have asked: "Why do you hate me?"

The question kept coming back, and even in the little sleep that overtook him just before daylight it continued to ask itself. No answer came, but an image did, repeated several times. For an interval seconds long, framed by utter darkness, she stood with malignant smoldering eyes trained squarely on his face.

He awakened in a sweat, in full daylight. He prepared a little breakfast and did not eat it, waiting. Still no warrant. Sunday, he remembered, and Mass at ten ... and surely the last one for him.

With God's help and only one acolyte and nine parishioners present, he managed it well enough. His homily, based on John 3:16, made no mention of his troubles. All received the Body and Blood from his hand and afterward wished him well. He returned to his quarters a little comforted and for a while refused, as he had refused all morning, to look at the newspaper lying on his doorstep. But the time had come, he picked it up. Not headlined but the front page had it, prominent enough: "Priest To Be Served Warrant." He did not read the story.

But still no warrant arrived and when finally he made his call it was only to learn that the matter was not yet decided. He prayed for most of an hour in the church, on his knees at the Virgin's shrine, and was back in his quarters just in time for a call from the diocese. A representative would arrive tomorrow, and Father Riley, if all went well, must come with him back to Atlanta. It was Chief Bostick, that just man, who had got in touch with the bishop.

This was better news but better still was something that happened later. Just before sunset he was wakened from a fitful nap by a knocking at his door. It was a group of his parishioners, eight of them, led by Thomas Bollen and his wife. They had brought food, a feast, lamb fresh roasted and rice, baked apples, yeasty rolls, and a bottle of white wine...all things they had somehow known were to his taste. He made shift to seat them, fetching two more chairs and a stool out of the kitchen, placing them so as to complete a circle. After grace, the one he favored from all those he remembered, they ate and drank together, speaking only of pleasant and often laughable things: of picnics differently recalled, of a bumbling first-time acolyte, of the day when Henry Flynn came staggering drunk to Mass. At last, with things put back in order by the women, they received his blessing and one by one stepped forward to shake his hand. Clearly they knew as well as did he that this would be the last time.

This was true but true in a different sense, a sense far graver than Father Riley had reason to imagine. Anticipating tomorrow, he spent a while packing his clothes and books and his few other personal items. Then he sat down to think. The light hurt his eyes and he turned it off and sat in the dark, thinking. He had not meant to go to sleep, but he did, seated in his chair. He might have been asleep for a long time before he waked up suddenly. At first he thought it was a sound that had waked him. Then he recognized that it was the smell of smoke: something was afire. He lurched up from his chair and out the door. It was the church. He ran.

The firemen found him inside the burning church, on the floor with his clothes afire, still holding on to a chalice and a silver crucifix. They carried him out just ahead of the flames, those objects still in his grip. He was terribly burned, fatally it appeared. While waiting for the ambulance they noticed something else. He had a wound, indented in his head, obviously from some kind of implement. The police, piecing things together, came up with a scenario. The arsonists, which they clearly were, had been surprised, had struck him down with something like a crowbar, and immediately fled. But he had partly recovered and somehow had managed to make his way into the church, where the firemen found him. As to the identity of the arsonists, no clue had been discovered. The victim, who had looked as if he might not survive even so short a trip, had been sent by ambulance to the regional hospital.

14

It happened that Hugh, returning about midnight from a visit out of town, passed close enough to notice the glow of light among distant trees. He knew it was a fire, some building, but it was a moment before his mind could settle on the spot. Then he knew. He touched his brakes but almost too fast took the upcoming turn.

There was not much left to see. The entire roof and most of the walls lay in a rubble of smoking hissing embers, in shuddering light from bursts of flame and clouds of ashes swirled about by streams from the firemen's hoses. A little back in the edge of darkness, illumined and faint by turns, a crowd of faces looked on silently. Hugh among them broke his own silence at last. To the old man standing next to him he said, "How did it start?"

"By somebody's hand, they say. Wasn't no accident."

Hugh looked around through the crowd, looked at the little house out back where light inside gave shape to the windows. "Was Father Riley here?"

The old man looked up at him, a dim but vaguely familiar face, perhaps a man Hugh once had known. He said, "Yeah. He was here. Wish to God he hadn't of been."

Something tightened in Hugh's throat. "What do you mean?"

"He was in there."

"In what? . . . In the fire?"

"Yeah. They got him out all burnt."

Hugh, though stopped hard for a second, murmured, "Dead?"

"Same as." The voice, when it came again, seemed thin as a far-off whisper in Hugh's ear: "They taken him off in a ambulance half hour ago. Don't give him no real chance."

There was a long space in which these words, though clear enough in Hugh's mind, seemed to resist understanding, and it was a while yet before he could quite get hold of them. In the meantime, with some part of his attention, his gaze had settled on the one still-standing segment of the wall, a rear corner including one of the windows. There appeared to be glass still there, an illumined fragment in the pointed arch at the top of the window frame. Finally he changed his position, moved closer. He was right, it was what he had thought and what he had vaguely hoped to see: the head though without a body now of Christ ascending to heaven.

His head was clear by now and the thought of that ambulance sent him straight to his car. He reached the hospital just in time, for the ambulance with gate door open stood waiting in the lighted breezeway at the emergency entrance. Amid the little cluster of men already making way, he watched the stretcher carried slowly down a ramp from the building door. Though wrapped in the whiteness of sheet and bandages, half the face was exposed, and Hugh in a moment of pause could see that this one eye was open. Quickly stepping forward, leaning down, "Father John," he murmured. He thought he saw the eye blink. An acknowledgment, he hoped, and watched as they lifted and placed the stretcher inside the ambulance. And that was all. It was on its way to Atlanta.

He got what details there were to be had and conversed for a minute or two with Dr. Tate. "All those goddamn rumors," Tate said. "No life in this town but gossip. Uglier the better."

"Maybe those motorcycle boys?" Hugh said.

"Could be. They'll have to find somebody to blame. Hope it's the right ones."

Hugh got in his car and drove slowly away, then turned aside for one more look at the smoldering ruin of the church. At home he went first to the kitchen and poured a drink. Pondering, he finished it off before he went upstairs.

She was not asleep. A light was on and there was faint music from the radio on the bedside table. Propped up in bed, in one of her sheer gowns, putting aside her magazine she looked up at him. Her dark eyes seemed to register something. What?

"All right," she said. "Tell me."

"You haven't heard, I suppose."

She only waited, the reading look in her dark eyes.

"You're rid of my beloved priest."

She blinked, but the look was still there. "How so?"

"Somebody set his church on fire. He went in to try and save some things, and got caught. They dragged him out of the fire."

She blinked again. "Dead?"

"Not yet, quite. They don't think he'll get to Atlanta alive."

A small movement of her lips preceded her words. "I'm sorry. An awful thing."

Surely she must have meant it. "Yeah. Pretty awful. Like him or not." Then, taking off his coat, he said, "Believe me, though, he was a good man. Faithful."

"I believe you." But her tone was not quite to his liking.

Then his tie. Feeling that her gaze followed him he undressed and finally stood there in his pajamas. He said, "I think he was conscious when I spoke to him. One of his eyes wasn't bandaged over and it was open. It blinked when I spoke to him. I think he heard me." There was silence. "He believes in miracles. Maybe there'll be one to save him."

There was silence still. When he looked at her it was squarely into the gaze fastened upon him. "Fastened" was the word, for it did not in those seconds turn aside. A typical challenge, he first thought, to what he had just now said. Then he thought that somehow there was more to it. But what?

"Who do they think did it?" she said.

"No clues. Not yet . . . But I guess you could say `all of us.'"

"All of us," she repeated, an edge to her voice. "Including you. Baring your breast. You and your stupid guilt. What good is it."

"Seems human to me."

A flicker of a smile. "I guess I'm not human, then, I'm glad to say. I chucked all your superstitions when I was still a child."

"Too bad," he started to say and changed his mind. He went into the bathroom.

When he came out the light was off, the darkness faintly relieved by glow from a half-moon in the west. Lying down in silence beside her he was instantly conscious of her perfume. Meant, no doubt, to invite him, he reckoned, though this before he came home. The thought was repugnant to him now, his body lying as stiff and cold as if in the chill of winter. She stirred; her hand like ice lay on him When he did not move, the hand withdrew and silence gathered around them.

In time, still sleepless, he heard her breathing, and much later her muffled voice. It was like an unclear name she repeated, calling it in her sleep. Then stillness again and after a while he got up from the bed.

He paced, went downstairs, and after a lingering drink of whiskey came back up again. The moon, now directly poised in the frame of the west window, made a gloaming in the room. Her sleeping face was visible in shadowy detail, and suddenly his attention was fixed upon it. Something in her expression, by a trick of the light, perhaps, distressed him in a way he could not explain. It made him think of that blissful swoon that can follow intercourse.

15

AFTER SEVERAL DAYS there was still no definitive word about Father Riley. Alive, it was presumed, though hanging at death's door. A purely factual account of the event had appeared next day in the *Herald* and on the following day a somber editorial urging that the perpetrators be swiftly discovered and brought to justice. For the first time since his arrival in Lakepoint a local matter had compelled Wilbur Helton's attention.

One reason, surely, was the fact that it had touched in him a string not truly sounded in many years. The immediate occasion, on the evening after the event, was those first moments when he stood there viewing the burned-out ruins where the old church had been. Intermittent wisps of smoke still rose and drifted about. Like the returning memories, he thought, drifting random and ghostly through his mind. There were other onlookers, perhaps with just such memories, standing exiled and poignant along the stretch of police tape that encircled the ash and cinders. Straight across on the other side, the old graveyard in maple shade was clearly visible now. He walked around, passing in front of the little house where the priest had lived. He walked among the stones and found the family plot. At the center was a single stone, higher than his head, the chiseled names of his mother and father and others less well remembered. Old names now, old deaths, his mother's the last one of them all. He decided all of a sudden that his name would one day be among them.

To Wilbur's recollection he had never but once, and that from a distance, laid eyes on this priest. But what followed from his hour of reflection that evening amounted to a practical revision of this plain fact. He kept recalling the little house and then the church as it had been, envisioning the priest at his sacred duties: at Mass with the chalice in his hands, uplifted now, while the chiming bell proclaimed the truth that wine was changed to blood. This was the work of memory, of another time and priest, but somehow it made the difference. The man, priestly garb and all, had become an insistent presence in Wilbur's mind. Father Riley was his name.

Not that the difference itself could lead him to any foreseeable action. The result was only that now he felt involved and went his daily rounds with his ear cocked for any talk of the event. Surprisingly, however, there was little to hear. Even at the courthouse among lawyers and clients awaiting their time in court, mention of the subject rarely occasioned a more than muted response. There was one clear exception. From a little distance he overheard what amounted to an argument on the question of who was guilty. The opinionated voice of Bunny Simmons was dominant among them, proclaiming with the support of gestures his certainty in the matter. It was those kids, the gang with the bikes, who had been abroad that night. And more . . . The argument went nowhere, but Wilbur did hear one thing that before the day was over he discovered to be true. Those same boys even now were up for questioning by the police.

So it was that Wilbur, on his own business at the police station, guessed at once the identity of the two boys seated there . . . the last of the group still waiting their turns to be interviewed one by one. He too was required to wait, and in his chair directly across the otherwise nearly empty room he was positioned to look them over. Except that they sat with bowed heads close together, exchanging whispers, there was nothing special to see: no black skullcaps or baggy shirts about them any longer. One boy, in fact, had got a crew cut for the occasion, and the other, in spite of long hair and rings in his ears, had the look of anybody's regular high school junior.

"All right, Payton." The voice belonged to the policeman at the desk near an exit door. Payton was instantly on his feet, in motion, nervously clawing at his hair with crooked fingers, passing through the door that now the policeman held open for him. This left the crew-cut boy, who was sitting only half upright with his face propped in his hands.

A little later, from the nearby water fountain, the policeman said, "Be a while yet, Mr. Helton." Wilbur nodded and when he looked again the crew-cut boy was staring at him. Then the boy was up, a short muscular body, crossing the room, stopping in front of Wilbur. Quietly he said, "Are you the lawyer?"

"One of them," Wilbur said.

"Can I talk to you?"

"All right."

The boy sat down beside him and after a pause, in a muted wary voice, said, "They trying to lay it on us. That fire."

For a second Wilbur looked straight into his wide blue eyes. "Why do you think so? You're just here for questioning, aren't you?"

"They going to put it on somebody. Got us figured for pigeons. Just 'cause we been in trouble a few times. And ride around on bikes. All they need."

"What kind of trouble?" Wilbur said.

"Just little stuff. You know. But that business with that preacher wasn't nothing. We was just playing a game with him, scaring him a little bit. Everybody talked him down, about him doing it with little girls. Up till now, they did." As if in fear of hidden listeners, he paused and looked around. "That guy had to get burnt up to get one good word said about him. Now they going to make it up to him. See what I mean?"

"I see, all right. But they've got to have real evidence. Where are they going to get it?"

"Cook it up. They ain't got too holy for that yet. Like that new mayor, Baker. Him just barely in there after all that row about votes, already speechifying like a preacher. That's what put him in."

This was about right, Wilbur thought: peace in the valley. He said, "I haven't heard of him mentioning you boys, though."

"Got his eye on us, though. You can bet on it."

Wilbur, silent for a moment, looked squarely at him again. "Have you got any idea who might have done it?"

"Not really. Niggers, maybe."

"That's not likely. He was kind of their boy. You ought to know that."

The policeman had got up from his desk and the boy glanced warily at him. In a voice almost a whisper he said, "Maybe you could be lawyer for us?"

"Just wait and see," Wilbur said. "If they get serious with you, you can come see me at my office. I'm there..."

"It's your turn now, boy." This was the policeman's voice, and the boy instantly got to his feet. He took a step, then barely paused to say. "My name's Joe Pace." He went on and passed through the door.

Back in his office an hour later Wilbur thought that the person knocking softly at his own door would turn out to be the Pace boy. Once again he was pleasantly taken aback. Despite the warmth of his invitation he had been all but sure that her visit three weeks ago was a one-time thing. Here she was, however, in what appeared to be the same plain cotton dress, her hair as on the earlier visit surprisingly neglected. There was more than this to surprise, even bewilder him. It was her demeanor. It grew more pronounced as the minutes passed, time spent in halting questions and answers concerning trivial matters. Except for her lips and often-blinking eyelids she scarcely stirred. Her hands, tightly folded, seemed not so much at rest in her lap as compelled to keep their place. What did she want? He shifted his seat on the desk and, circling back, tried again.

"Everything all right at home?"

"Yes. Okay." But her eyes wandered away from him. "I'm still going to my dancing lessons."

"And doing well, I'll bet. Maybe you'll end up in New York. In some ballet group."

"I'd like that." Her gaze came back to him. "Do you remember you were the one that took me to my first dancing lesson. I was just eight." Her manner had softened.

"Sure I remember. You were pretty but a little plump then. Now you're slim and even prettier."

She smiled, her teeth a trifle uneven. There came a little change in her expression, a sort of letting go. She said, "I might be going away to school."

"Oh." He considered for a moment, weighing his question. "Don't you like your school here? No trouble or anything?"

With a decisiveness Wilbur had not looked for, she shook her head. "It's just . . . She thinks it would be good for me. A new place . . . And a better school, too."

To end the silence that had fallen, Wilbur said, "I can see why a new place might be better, considering things here."

But it did not break her silence. She was looking down at her hands, pretty hands though once again tensely locked together. Was it her mother, trouble, real trouble between them? In this moment, despite his feeling of tenderness for her, a bitter satisfaction took hold. She, that woman, sleek and cunning as a serpent, stood there in his mind's eye: thwarted, even confounded perhaps, for one time in her life. It was this that spurred him to flatly drop his attempts at artfulness. Squarely in her face he said, "There's something you want to tell me, Jean. Is it about your mother? You can tell me. I'm your father, who loves you."

Her face had gone pale. Her lips moved, just barely, but no words came. "You can tell me." Then, "I can keep a secret." Maybe he could.

Refusal again, the shaking of her head. "No. Please. I can't . . . Maybe . . ."

A shocking click and the door came open. It was Miss Miller, his secretary, stepping brightly into the room. Jean was on her feet. "Wait," Wilbur said . . . in vain because Jean was through the door and vanishing down the stairs. He hurriedly followed to the head of stairs and there had a change of mind. "Maybe . . ." This one last word of hers was left to linger in his memory.

To Miss Miller's puzzled face he said, "My daughter. Just a little tiff is all."

16

Nora at her dressing table sat listening, gazing with unfocused eyes at her image in the mirror. A full two hours now and Jean had not come back. From her high east window Nora had watched, seen her disappear among trees on the steep grade that mounted at last to the ridge top. There to stay and stay ... only, surely to brood. Dangerous brooding. How many times in these last days?

Nora, this once, had been obtuse, too sure of herself, counting on her power. Always this had been enough, and her failure had come as a shock. The sterner stuff of which she was made had not been passed to her daughter. The thought brought vexation, then anger again, but discretion was her habit. She consoled herself by supposing that time was bound to renew their union. But now ... ?

First to mind on that morning ten days ago was the question of how the news had got to Jean. But this, all too soon explained, was only the troubling preface to Nora's distress. Restless that night, Jean had been up and about, and from the head of the stairs, sharp-eared, had heard what her parents were saying. Even in small detail, it appeared, for she distinctly remembered that eye looking up at Hugh. This in fact was the special detail that had haunted the rest of her night.

When, after breakfast and Hugh's departure, Nora had come to rouse her, the look on her daughter's face was enough to stop the words in her mouth. Sick, she thought, and quickly approached with new words on her tongue. These too went undelivered, for suddenly, noting that Jean had turned her face away, Nora perceived her mistake. Uncertain now, she sat down on the foot of the bed. With the answer all but clear in her mind she quietly asked her question. "Tell me what's the matter, dear."

Nothing followed; Jean's face remained half hidden.

Finally, "Is it because you know what happened?"

No answer.

"How did you know?"

The answer came, barely came, no movement but her lips.

Spying, Nora thought, and put the thought aside. "I'm sorry you had to hear it that way. We're both so sorry, Hugh and I, about what happened. So terrible."

A little while and Jean's voice, faint almost as a whisper, said. "I dreamed about it. Things Hugh said. His eye."

In silence Nora picked among words that came and went in her mind. She said, "Please don't start imagining it's your fault, dear. So many people do that, feel guilty when they're not. It's so foolish. They'll find the ones that did it." Then, "If either one of us should feel guilty, it would be me." Suddenly uneasy she paused, scanned her memory for troublesome things she might have said to Hugh. "I only meant to do what was right. I couldn't keep quiet, could I, with something like that going on? Something I knew about. Could I, dear?"

She had to wait for an answer: a muted "No."

"Think about what I've said. You'll see. Everything will be all right."

It was time to hush. She stood up. "Go back to sleep, dear."

It was not all right. The silences between them, day by day, like nothing in Nora's memory, had not in any way diminished. She tried at first with little ploys, a tone to please and divert, but never with success. Hugh, slow to notice more subtle things and accustomed anyway to Jean's muteness in his presence, did not fail to notice this. "What's wrong with her, Nora?" he would ask, suspecting, as she discerned, that the girl was pregnant. This was vexing but useful for now and she let him keep his suspicion. For such vexation was nothing compared to her daily increasing distress. And what had been only distress for a while was close to becoming anger.

Then, in a single minute of revelation, it did become anger, a burst of it hard to suppress. Hugh, stopping by in the afternoon to retrieve some forgotten item, also brought a bit of news. It was about Jean, her visit to Wilbur's office, reported to Hugh by a casual friend who worked in that same building. Hugh, watching Nora's face, said, "I know how you feel," and turned and left. The least of her thoughts was that his demeanor had lacked real sympathy.

Afterward, the calmer for being seated at her dressing table, she saw it as good fortune that Jean had taken this time to be absent . . . absent and brooding on her hilltop. How much longer? It was getting late.

Her impatience brought her at last to a decision. She was calm enough to pause and put on walking shoes, thinking that this would be enough. She was badly wrong. From the house all the way up the long slope to the ridge top, only trees in foliage were visible, and she had envisioned nothing more than an easy walk among tree trunks. But there were vines, interlaced, and solid thickets of briers. A strange world, hostile to her, and she could find no path. Turn back? But she persisted, picking her way, embattled among the vines that seized her and thorns that snared her arms and skirt. Turn back? She would not. Strangely incensed, sweating from all her pores, she fought her way on and came at last to the clearing at the top.

A little before sunset, hair and clothes disheveled, with streaks of blood on her arms and hands, she stood there laboring for breath. To left and right along the stretch of bare ridge top, to enclosing thicket at either end, there was no one to be seen. No one, nothing, nothing green or growing, but only scattered and heaped up stones in the whole of this lifeless space. She was taken aback, strangely so. And next, for one appalling moment, she seemed to envision what had happened here, happened ages ago: a fiery blast, one titanic lightning strike, and all things turned to stone. Stones for graves, she thought, her gaze drawn haphazard to ones of fitting graveyard size.

The moment passed. Still panting, in a silence ruffled only by her breath, she sat down on a nearby stone. Soon the silence was perfect: no birds, no stirrings made by wind. And the town below, its full expanse, lay as inert and soundless as if engraved in the earth. She shook her head. Impatience gathered in her. Her eyes scouted the ridge once more and then looked down at her arms, her blouse. All this and all for nothing. Feeling her anger gather itself to a single pure moment of rage, she stood up suddenly. Beyond the town and the lake and the distant fields, the sun like a smoldering orange disc hung barely above the horizon. In a kind of entrancement she watched it, watched it slowly close and, touching now, ignite and then inflame the edge of the world. The words rose up and took shape on her lips in a whisper of secret command: "Burn it. Burn it all to a cinder."

She discovered a path and followed it. But halfway down, by some misstep, she lost it and found herself in confusion. She turned back. Then suddenly, in the dusky light, she felt herself snared as in a trap. A moment of panic took hold. There was a presence somewhere close by, with eyes intent upon her. They held her frozen there for a moment, before she mastered herself and breaking through vines came onto the path again. She drew a breath. Foolishness. But the thought did not clear her mind. She went on, not fast, containing her impulse to hurry. Followed, stalked? The question went unanswered until she stepped out free of the woods.

There was light in the house but no one in sight when she entered and went up to Jean's room. The door was shut. She drew a breath. She opened the door and saw her daughter, a startled look on her face. Then, seconds later, "Mama. What happened to you?"

The thought of her own appearance only glanced across Nora's mind. "I went to look for you," she said. "I got off the path. Sit down."

She did, on the bed, her wide eyes fixed on her mother.

Half aware of the challenge in her voice, Nora said, "I learned something. That you went to visit Wilbur. Why?" She did not like the flustered look on Jean's face. "What did you say to him?"

"Nothing. We just talked."

Her expression and faltering voice were not convincing. "Tell me what you talked about."

"Only just things, things we remembered. I didn't say anything about . . . that."

Nora paused. "You just went there to reminisce? Don't lie to me."

Shaking her head, "Please, Mama. I never have lied to you."

Nora thought that this was true . . . at least until this moment. She studied Jean's face, a little averted now, and pale. She thought of these recent days, the girl's evasive, secret manner . . . so different, brooding. Disheveled dress and hair also, just as she looked now. Even her room was disordered, that used to be neat and bright.

Nora sat down in the chair close by. A moment more of study and she said, "Why would you go to him? You never liked him."

Jean's face was still averted. Quietly, "I don't know. I guess . . . I guess I was just feeling lonesome or something."

"What about me? You've always talked to me, about things."

Jean was a long time answering and then her words were nearly inaudible. "It's different."

"What's different, dear?"

Finally, "Us."

What Nora felt was a curious mix of hurt and anger together. "Why would you say that?" She waited, in vain. "You don't trust me anymore, is that it? But I told you the truth . . . when we talked about all that. Don't you remember what I said?" She added, "It's false guilt, dear."

No answer.

A flash of unmixed anger made Nora say, "I'll go ahead and make inquiries about a school. That's what you want, isn't it?"

Jean looked glancingly at her. "I'm sorry, Mama," she whispered.

Nora stood up, her eyes still fastened on the girl. No longer pretty, that face, she thought . . . it had been but the flush of youth. Nora hesitated, then said, "In the meantime, stay away from Wilbur. You don't know what he's really like. But I do." She turned and left.

In her own room she stood with clenched hands at her sides, feeling her anger rise above, obliterate her pain . . . her pain and just for the moment something else besides. The something was fear without a name that lurked like a presence nearby. Turning, she faced the mirror and saw the figure her daughter had seen: a stranger in shabby and savage disarray, with actual blood on her arms and hands.

17

AFTER MORE THAN TWO WEEKS it was still the case that no official word about Father Riley had been received. Nevertheless it was said by those who seemed to know that he had died, an opinion now generally accepted. This was so far true that already there was a plan afoot aimed at making amends. It was, at community expense, to rebuild the church. The idea was Hugh's, who, without so much as a hint to Nora, had brought it to Mayor Baker and persuaded him. His plan was now up for approval by the city council.

Also afoot, and related to this, was the public pressure on the police and other officials to discover the perpetrators. With no other credible suspects, the motorcycle boys, the "Black Caps," were more and more in the public eye. So it was that Chief Bostick, still at the helm, dispatched his two detectives on a mission that he regarded as wasted days, scouring the crime scene, interviewing, quizzing potential witnesses who appeared to believe what they said: that they had heard the sound of motorcycles not far from the church that night; that suspicious scraps of conversation had come to them through their children; that one of the gang had cut his hair because the fire had singed it. Bostick's experience had made him accustomed to the like, but this was a special instance—so many witnesses, earnest faces, as eager as drummers to make it plain that their hearts were in the matter. And there, exerting no little pressure of his own, was Bernie Golden, both district attorney and self-appointed conscience of the people. He at least seemed prepared to bring charges against some or all of the boys.

But whatever Golden really meant to do, the word was out, and Wilbur was not surprised when on a Monday afternoon the Pace boy, with his father in tow, appeared for a consultation. In his office with the door shut behind them, they sat uncomfortably in chairs across the desk from Wilbur, silent at first, waiting on him. Except for his bulk and short-cut hair the boy resembled his father: blue eyes, pug nose, thin lips compressed as if to contain urgent words in their mouths. Then, "I come along 'cause he wanted me to," the father said. "I don't know nothing about the law, I'm a bricklayer. But I sho' know this boy never set that fire."

"I was at my gal's house that night. Go ask her. Name's Lily Banks. Lives out on the Cotter road."

"This boy's done some bad stuff, I grant you," the father said. "But burning down no church ain't one of them. He . . ."

Wilbur with some firmness put a stop to it, explaining and then explaining again that they were ahead of the game, describing how it worked, that they must wait for formal charges that might just as well not come. He had got them silenced and at the verge of standing up when he thought to ask a question. It was one he had asked before, at the police station. To the boy he said, "Are you sure you don't have even a notion who might have done it? Heard talk or anything? Like about the priest. Mean talk."

The boy blinked. "Aw I heard talk, all right. Plenty of it. Some of it mean . . . along with making jokes. Gals was the meanest . . . when they wasn't giggling."

"But nothing special, that sticks in your mind?"

"Can't think of none."

"Okay," Wilbur said. "If you do think of anything, come tell me." He stood up.

The two of them followed, were on their feet when suddenly he had another thought. It came because she was fast in his mind and had been so for days. "Do you know Jean Helton? A little younger than you, maybe."

"Yeah. A little bit. A fancy dancer."

Another thought presented itself. "Was she in on the talk, the giggling. Just curious."

"I can't recollect she was. Stand-offish like. She's bound to been around it, though. She kin to you?"

"Yeah," Wilbur said, and waited and then they were gone.

Because of this, the thought of Jean, it seemed a bit more than a coincidence when, on his way for a talk with Bostick, he happened to see her standing on the sidewalk. He quickly parked his car and she was still there, gazing into a window where garments were on display . . . she in the same brown rumpled dress, or one that looked just like it. She did not see him approaching; in fact, judging by her listless posture, she was not seeing anything, not even the garments there before her eyes. But she came to life when she saw him, a shock that set her back a step.

"Jean," he said. "I've been hoping you'd come to see me again."

A quick glance over her shoulder and with eyes gone bright for a second she looked back at him. Afraid? Of him? "I can't," she faintly said.

He had to take this in. "Because of your mother, you mean?"

She gave that sideways glance again, then opened her mouth to speak. A man walked past. Wilbur said, "Come on, let's go get a Coke."

"Mama's in there." She meant, by a gesture more of eyes than head, the beauty parlor next door.

But she was wrong. Mama was there on the walk, standing upright and rigid in her elegance, crowned by the sculptured upswept coif of her blue-black hair in the sun. It was Wilbur who held her gaze, a look he hoped he need never confront a second time in his life. In a voice like ice she said, "Jean. Come on."

Jean went and at her mother's side set off down the walk. But only for a few steps. Nora stopped and turned around. Again, that look. "Let my daughter alone," she said and left him standing there.

For what might have been quite a while, pedestrians like so many shadows passing him by, he stood there in thought. The sound of a horn shook him out of it and he went back to his car.

There were others with business at the police station that day and Wilbur had to wait most of an impatient and troubled hour to see Chief Bostick. Actually it was a waste of time (like most of his hours) for he was the same as sure there was nothing new. This was his first question to Bostick and the answer was as expected. "Nope. You know as much as I do. Which is that them boys sho'ly didn't do it."

He was comfortable with Bostick, had been from the first, and his two or three conversations with the old man, here in this little office behind the shut door, had by now established a certain intimacy between them.

"Naw," he went on. "This town. They couldn't say enough bad things about that poor fellow. Run him down till a fly wouldn't light on him. First time in twenty years they all agreed about anything. Then him and his church both got burnt up and look at them now."

He looked tired, Wilbur thought, a little older and the tremor more pronounced than before. "I know," he said.

"I would sho'ly like to find out the ones did it, though. Mean thing. Ugly. That little church been standing there near a hundred years." He put a hand, surprisingly fit and supple, on the desk and drummed with his fingers.

"And still nothing to go on," Wilbur murmured.

"Naw. That poor fellow. I'm glad I got that warrant put off. Bad enough him thinking it was on the way." He drummed with his fingers again.

"And you're still sure he wasn't guilty?"

"I was about sure to start with. Hysterical woman. It ain't nothing gossip can't make happen." He paused. "She didn't hardly know what a warrant was. Somebody told her to come to me."

"Who?" Wilbur said.

"I asked her that. She just said it was somebody that knew about the law."

"No name?"

"Naw. Just a friend, was all she said. I didn't see no need to push her."

But Nora was in Wilbur's mind, Nora standing there on the walk with assassin's eyes trained on him. In fact she was still there when he left the police station and sat in his parked car with the motor idling. Improbable, he thought, an effect of those moments with Jean and her, back there on the sidewalk. But once he had set the car in motion he knew where he was headed.

He had to stop at a public phone booth and consult the book. He found Bass Street and driving slowly came to the box that had the McDougal number. There was a For Sale sign in the yard. He turned in, among azalea bushes, and parked in the shade of a massive oak. Deserted looking, but he mounted onto the wide, roofed porch and knocked at the door. A hollow sound and he knocked again. There was nothing, no chair or swing, on the porch or in the yard. He walked around and looked into an empty garage. He went next door and asked. He was told that Mrs. McDougal, without explanation, had moved out more than a week ago. As to where she had gone the neighbor knew only that it was to someplace at a good distance from Lakepoint.

18

DAY BY DAY Nora's behavior had become more perplexing, more disturbing to Hugh. Perhaps he had been slow to notice, but in his mind he dated its beginning from that morning at the breakfast table. Her hands and arms, those scratches, a network from elbows down. "What the devil happened?" he said.

She did not even glance at them. Without looking at him, either, she said, "Those briers up the hill there. I got caught in them."

A puzzle to start with, that she to whom woods and briers were as strange as Egypt's pyramids should be up there at all. "What were you doing up there?"

"I went to find Jean. I was worried about her. I missed the path."

"Why? She goes up there a lot, doesn't she?"

"Not for so long."

Almost satisfied, he said, "Well, you'd better put something on those scratches," and got no answer.

Worried about her. These remembered words were part of what soon led him to his tentative conclusion that the girl was pregnant. He knew of course that Nora had been angered by her visit to Wilbur. But this alone, he felt, could not account for Nora's behavior toward her, a radically different behavior. Perhaps it was both things together, each one, to her mind, a sort of betrayal, a threat to the binding, the excessive, intimacy they had shared. This would explain it, he had thought, and only wondered that she consistently evaded, with skill and determination, his attempts to pry. After all, as to the matter of the girl's pregnancy, in these times and given Nora's views, abortion could not have been a simpler answer.

But days went by and the only change was that he had become increasingly aware of something still harder to explain: an often withering coldness toward the girl that caused him real discomfort. Orders flatly given, few endearments now, and a haunting sense that the bond between them had become an invisible leash. Only once, in Jean's absence, had he dared make a persistent effort to intrude. The response, the look of seething anger she had finally trained on him, was only a part of the reason he had not risked a second try. For what afterward fixed itself in his mind was the nebulous impression that he had stood face-to-face with a person no longer known to him. A gulf, he thought, growing between them, that he could not reach across.

On a Sunday afternoon when he could count on Nora's absence for an hour, he made up his mind to stick his neck out. He climbed the steps and walked down the hall to Jean's room. As always her door was shut. Though he knew she was in there, his gentle knock was not answered. "Jean," he said, "it's Hugh." No answer. "Could I talk to you for just a minute?" Finally he heard a footstep and then a click of the latch. She was looking up at him, discomfort plain in her face. "Can I come in?" he said. "Just for a minute?" She opened the door for him.

Thinking it might help he said, "Can I sit down? Your mother's gone out for a little while."

At her nod he sat on the chair close by, but Jean did not follow his lead. From a little distance she stood not quite looking at him, her expression something between uncertainty and distrust. All around her was disarray: an unmade bed, scattered garments, a window curtain half detached from its rod. He said, "I wish you could think of me as a friend . . . that you can trust. Because you can trust me."

There was a slight movement like a ripple in her expression, then nothing, silence. He wondered if she was listening in fear of her mother's return.

"I can tell there's something wrong between you and your mother. I might be able to help. I can keep my mouth shut, too."

No response, just that dimly haggard face gazing perhaps at the door beside him. No use. But suddenly, brightening, she said, "I'll be going off to school pretty soon."

"Oh?" he said and seconds later, seeing her changed, her fallen expression, regretted what he had revealed.

"You didn't know? Mama didn't tell you?" She was all intentness now, anxiety behind it.

"I believe she did," he said, trying to counter his gaffe. "I'd forgotten." But he saw in her gaze that she was already conscious that he was lying. Uselessly he said, "It just slipped my mind."

Turned away from him, her face was hard to read. But then she said, "Please. I think Mama's back."

He had heard nothing. But now, once more, he heard her urgent "Please" and was moved to get up quickly and go downstairs. It was no real surprise when he found that Nora had not returned.

All this and no answers had now become a more than disturbing preoccupation. Sometimes it waked him in the night, persisting until he got out of bed and went downstairs for a drink. Or again, as on this Friday night that followed his talk with Jean, he simply stood at one of the bedroom windows looking out. On this occasion there was a full moon, its light suffusing and melding the landscape, drawing his gaze far into the murky distance. At times he ceased to look and only listened, conscious of Nora's breathing that seemed to fill the room around him. How deeply she slept, as deep as death . . . as if in death a body could find a way to go on breathing. But now and again as in nights past she murmured in her sleep: stifled words he vainly tried to make clear in his mind. Some were repeated, he thought or imagined . . . words for something she wanted? Perhaps, but it was not him she wanted. This much, he had come to believe, was all but a certainty now. Was it his personal failure . . . among other things, as a lover? Or was it what he suspected: that from the first her eye had been on his wealth and social standing. From rags to riches, to all those expensive garments and jewelry she had bought, to guaranteed respect in any quarter where she moved. And not least, of course, confirmed assurance of her dear daughter's prospects . . . Until now? This was strange.

He was suddenly very tired but for yet a little while at his window he went on thinking of these things and of how it had been, or seemed, in their early days. Her eagerness in bed: was it counterfeit, as now, disguised to near perfection by her skillful mimicry? He did not want to think so, not at the expense of remembered moments he valued with the best and warmest of his life. In any case the fault was hers, who in so short a time had contrived to escape beyond his reach. And even Jean's, a thing that was stranger still.

Why? A mystery without an answer, he thought, or none that was yet in sight.

But an answer of a certain kind was even now at hand. It was a thought that had never crossed his mind before this, but after what was soon to happen, it lingered on as a troublesome, a fragile explanation.

He finally turned from the window and like an intruder stealing in took his place in the bed beside her. But sleep did not come, her breathing kept it at bay. She stirred and murmured something . . . impossible to translate. Then again but louder, like a muffled cry in her throat. Her body came hard against him, her circling arm, her thigh. Her whispered voice, as if between clenched teeth: "Fuck me. Fuck me Now!" Her hot wet lips, her open mouth, fastened on his own.

Then, all in one instant of violent recoil, it was over. She lay with open eyes that stared straight up at the ceiling, still but for the now-declining harshness of her breath. He lay there as mute as she, groping for words, for meaning, conscious of a dim revulsion starting to take hold.

She got up. He watched her pass in shadow-light to the closet nearby. There she hesitated (thinking what? Of something to say, some kind of explanation?) and finally took a dressing gown and with never a word left the room. He could barely hear her naked feet on the stairs and wondered where she meant to go. Then through his confusion the word "lover" surfaced again. But to go with bare feet, in the night, in a dressing gown? It made no sense. Leaving the bed he stopped in the doorway and stood for a long time listening.

At last he went down and in the deeper darkness here made his way to the back door. The moon though setting gave light enough and he could see both cars parked outside the garage. He was ready to close the door when the thought struck him: it had not been locked. Had he simply forgot, forgot it this one time? The thought was enough to hold him there, mulling the question, his gaze scanning the half-lit lawn and the woods like a curtain of darkness. Now he had ceased to think about the lock. Was there a shape, a movement there against the backdrop of woods? He stepped outside and stopped and then went on. Halfway there he stopped again. It was only deceptive light and too much staring. He turned back, but with a nagging sense that he was in retreat. Inside, after another pause, he shut and locked the door.

The guest room, of course. Approaching it softly, he reached and found the door knob. Locked. He stood there until half-assured that he could hear her breathing. He went back to his bed but did not sleep before dawn was at the windows.

᎒ ᎒ ᎒

He overslept and waking to the sound of rain could tell that it was late. Confront her now? Maybe Jean would be with her, making this impossible. Uncertain what to do or say, he got up slowly and slowly dressed. A glance revealed that Jean's door was shut. He thought of waking her, of using her presence to postpone the question he had to ask. Or not ask? Maybe he would wait, and watch, and find that he was mistaken. With a foolish stealth he went down the stairs.

She was not in the house but he was in time to see her, from the kitchen, get into her car and turn it around and drive away out of sight. Where, in this rain now falling heavy? For a while he sat at the table thinking, thinking at last of Jean. He noticed that the stove clock said eleven and he wondered if she was still there in her room. He would see, and maybe this time, with luck, be able to draw her out. Finally he rose from his chair and went upstairs to her door.

He knocked, and then again, and then again. No sound within. Not there? He called her name. He put his hand on the knob, then paused and called again. No answer. He opened the door.

He knew at once that her stillness, her body lying faceup on the bed as if it had been dropped there, was not the stillness of normal sleep. A few quick strides and he was beside her, bending down. Her eyes were shut, her mouth half open. With his hand on her breast, "Jean," he said. She was barely breathing, troubled breath. "Jean," he said again, but she lay as before. On the bedside table a small bottle caught his eye. He recognized it, picked it up. It was empty now . . . of Nora's sleeping tablets.

He did the thing that came to mind. He heaved her up in his arms and staggering at times descended the stairs and carried her out as fast as he could to his car.

19

THERE WAS A SMALL RESTAURANT down on Water Street where, because it was little frequented during the day, she often went for an idle time over coffee. It was where she had come this morning, in rain from black clouds thickening overhead, on impulse spurred by the consciousness of Hugh's approaching footsteps. A flight, in fact, for she had not felt able to put on the face she needed. Even now, in her booth in the restaurant, she noticed the trembling of her hand when she reached for the coffee cup. Weakness. She deplored it. For wasn't this what she wanted: the girl dead, dead or dying?

In her kitchen an hour, two hours ago, with a jolting turn of mind to this new distraction, she had noticed the silence all around and thought what it could mean. The sleeping tablets, gone from her cabinet shelf since yesterday . . . not one or two but all. And at once she knew, had to know, what hand had taken them. In the rigid stillness now, enforced by the silent kitchen clock that said almost eleven, she had got up from her chair.

At the foot of the stairs she paused, removed her shoes. Reaching the top she could see that Hugh was still asleep in the bed. Then down the hall with soundless feet to the shut door of Jean's room. She stopped, listened. With her hand on the knob she waited, then ever so slowly turned it. A little crack, then wider. At once she knew, or believed she did, for what she saw stretched out on the bed did not have the look of repose. A dangling arm, lips too wide apart. Dead? A tingling chill swept upward from her spine. She took a cautious step or two and stood transfixed near the bed. No sign of breath. And there on the table, overturned, the empty bottle lay. Two steps back and then one more brought her against the doorjamb. Soundlessly she shut the door and stole away down the hall. Back in the kitchen, with shoes in hand, she stood, then sat and waited, waited on and on. Until she heard a distant stirring and Hugh's feet on the stairs.

In the restaurant booth she came to notice that there were two cups of coffee there in front of her now, both cold, one but half consumed. Was it the waiter whose eyes were on her? . . . no customer but herself. His back was turned and yet she knew that she was being watched. Her shifting gaze stopped suddenly, on a shape at the plate glass window. It was not fully distinct. In hooded colorless raincoat, in falling rain, the figure suggested a shape composed of the dim cloud light around it. This was a moment when Nora imagined that her eyes were playing a trick. It quickly passed, expelled by the surge of blood that came with the rising strokes of her heart. She knew who it was, could tell that it was "him." A discernible movement, an obscurely beckoning motion of his hand called Nora onto her feet. "Lady." The waiter's voice without effect followed her to the door.

Out in the deserted street, in the soaking rain she stopped. He was not there. In a moment of growing panic she looked to left and right and saw, it seemed, through the curtain of rain a spectral figure moving on, drawing away from her. She hurried. She thought he paused and beckoned and she would overtake him. But there was a corner and when she arrived, there was nothing to be seen. A few steps more and she stopped and stood there in the rain.

A man with a big umbrella approached from across the street. He stopped beside her and said, "It's room for two under here, ma'am." She heard and shook her head. "No bother," he said and she shook her head again. For a moment he hesitated, then crossed the street once more.

Mere nerves, an hallucination? It was too real, too relentlessly set, engraved upon her mind's eye. At last she turned and started back. Where an awning overhead had kept the pavement almost dry she stopped and searched for footprints. Her own were faintly discernible but it seemed to her there were others . . . larger prints made by feet no less substantial than hers. She went on. She entered the restaurant and, taking her purse from the booth, with a hand not fully in her control paid the silent waiter. One thing for just a second or two interrupted her departure. It was her reflection there in the window glass, the stark pale face offset by hair that hung like rat tails dripping.

She drove home slowly in slackening rain and paused before she turned in. That Hugh's car was not there brought her comfort of sorts, but a comfort that was short-lived. In the silent house, at the foot of the stairs, the tension seized her again. She collected herself, drew a breath and set out up the stairs.

Jean's door was open. There on the threshold, blood still stroking heavy in her neck, Nora looked into an empty room, at a bed with covers awry, at the table where the small bottle lay, overturned as before. Slowly her blood receded. There would be a message on the recorder, she thought, then thought it could wait a bit. She turned and went to her room.

Her mood had changed, turned upside down. In removing her sodden clothes she imagined the act of peeling away an old dead skin from her body. She rubbed her hair dry and combed and combed it and put on everyday clothes. Then to her mirror. All restored, she thought: gone the ugly pallor and moiled rat-tail hair. The message. Downing her little rush of panic she stepped to the telephone and with a cool hand pressed the button. Hugh's voice. At the hospital, come quick, your daughter . . . and this was all. She drew a breath and after a moment picked up her purse from the table.

But something loomed, some threatening thing at the edge of her consciousness. She stood there in thought and seemed to recall a notepad on the floor. Her body stiffened. Always, it was said, such people left some kind of written word. She dropped her purse and hurried.

It was there, on the floor beside the bed. She picked it up. There were words, just a few, but for a second her eyes refused to focus. Then, "Im sorry father because I . . ." and nothing more. She tore out the page and wadded it in her hand.

But something else had struck her mind. Visible where that page had been was the torn-off edge of another not in sight. She scanned the floor, the bed, got down on her knees and got up with her eyes fastened on the table. A long cold moment followed, for there, conspicuous on the lower shelf, was an open box of envelopes and stamps in a little book. Once again from Nora's own stores, sneaking in the night. And the mailbox . . . maybe? She turned and left in violent haste and went out through the drizzling rain.

There was nothing in the box . . . nor on the ground around it. Had he come, the mailman, maybe delayed by the rain? She stood there for minutes thinking, watching the road down the hill. She must do something. What? Then she remembered that she was expected and that she must go there first.

She drove fast and left her car in the space where the doctors parked. First to the information desk, then on to the elevator. She stood waiting. Why the rush when neither the girl's life nor death would bring that letter back? The door slid open, closed behind her; she stood in unexpected gloom. Someone was there, a figure beside her that murmured close to her ear: "Don't worry. I'll be with you."

Her throat went tight. "You . . ." she said.

But the door came open. Two men were awaiting her exit. She stepped out.

Then there was Hugh, through a doorway, rising from his chair. Approaching her now with a solemn face he paused for an instant, then softly said, "I'm sorry. She died a while ago."

Nora could not speak.

"From a lot of sleeping pills. Most of the bottle, I think. Yours, I guess." He got no answer. Finally, "Come sit down. You're pale as a ghost."

He took her arm and walked her to a chair in the waiting room and sat beside her. She knew she should speak, say something, but her mind was cloudy. "Don't worry," "he" had said. When her throat had loosened a little she faintly said, "They must have been mine. From our bathroom."

Hugh did not answer. He looked as if he wanted to say something, but he did not. A doctor came and gravely explained, holding her hand while he spoke. Did she wish to view the body? Nora hesitated. What was expected? In the end she shook her head, muttering that she could not.

20

Nora sat on the edge of the bed simply staring, a stare in no way interrupted when she answered Hugh's question. "No funeral," she said. "I want her cremated."

Except by the decisiveness of her voice he was not surprised. "All right. But there ought to be something. A small memorial service maybe. Or something. For the look of things, if nothing else."

"No. I want it over with. As quick as possible." Her eyes had the look of eyes planted in her head, in a face that was sickly pale. "Tell them now," she added.

He could understand her feelings but this decision did not sit well with him. It was too much as though a pet animal had died. Nevertheless with a mumbled "All right" he turned and went to use the telephone downstairs.

For at least the past two hours, observing her rigid expression, the moments when her fingers twitched or gathered in a fist, his unwillingness to intrude had kept him putting off this question. For surely this was grief without display, grief of a kind fitted to harrow the most obdurate soul. Blaming herself... and rightly so, he thought, recalling her strange and wanton cruelty to the girl... A cruelty consummated, however, by his own innocent gaffe of yesterday. This and the change it had brought about in the poor girl's expression was something he would be bound to remember for all the rest of his life.

And yet, vaguely enshrouding all his thoughts, there was a cloud of doubt. Had there not been more, some secret thing behind her treatment of Jean? A lover, he thought once more, somehow implicated? But who?... and where was any evidence he could put a finger on? For now he put these thoughts aside and picked up the telephone.

When he went back upstairs with the word that it was done he found her still seated on the bed, but not as before. She astonished him. A different face looked up at him, eyes with a soft and almost pleading look, and said, "At least I have only you to love now. Because I do love you, Hugh. Maybe I haven't always shown it; I've seemed cool sometimes, I know. But I won't be anymore." Her parted lips, a little pale, were being offered to him.

He could not respond. Something at the back of his mind raised a troubling question, and though he had bent a little forward he as quickly drew back. Devious words, a lie? Instinct and reason together were telling him this was so. She blinked. Turning her face away she said, "I'll prove it to you. You'll see."

What to make of it? He stood at the front window looking out and saw two cars approach and stop near the gate. They were getting out, two couples properly dressed. He said, "They're coming. The news has already got about."

Maybe she had not heard him. She said, "She was pregnant, you know. You were right."

A lie. He turned and confronted her. "No she wasn't. I asked the doctor."

Her gaze drifted away. "I thought she was."

He went down alone to greet the people and other friends who came after, friends whose visits he was at pains to prolong as much as he could. Until he was left alone again with thoughts that kept returning.

He put off going upstairs. In the kitchen he puttered at making supper and ended sitting at the table with a bottle of scotch at hand. He did not know how long but it was nearly dark when the telephone rang. He counted the rings, five of them, then languidly reached and took up the receiver.

At first, because it was strained and broken, he did not recognize the voice. Then, as the words began to come clear, he knew with a certain baffled agitation that it was his brother, Wilbur, and that the distortion in the voice was the sound of tearfulness. His daughter, he had heard it only now. Yes, Hugh thought, "his" daughter after all. It seemed strange, and not until he put the phone down was he quite certain what was wanted of him and what he had agreed to. But afterward it was mostly clear, especially the fact that he had promised to meet with Wilbur tomorrow. At nine o'clock, the office, his own. Through the haze of many drinks his mind kept returning to this.

But finally there was a problem. A hand heavy on his shoulder had restored a certain clarity. She was there looking down at him, her face rigid with anger. "You are not going to meet him. I heard on the phone upstairs."

Despite the sluggishness of his tongue he managed to say, "Why not?"

"That vicious, hateful man. A liar, he'll tell you lies. He hates me."

He brought himself to say, "She's his daughter."

She hesitated, no change in her face. "Even that's not true. He was not her father."

It took Hugh a moment to get it clear. "I never heard that before."

"It's true. I didn't see any reason to tell you."

True? He finally said, "Who was her father?"

"Someone you never knew." She started to leave, then stopped. "I'll never forgive you if you go."

"A lover," he said. "Do you have one now?"

A perceptible flicker or trick of her eyes was her response to this. In indignation she turned her back and left him there with his bottle.

But in the morning, in spite of her silent, her watchful presence, a little late and with throbbing head, he went. Wilbur was there, standing on the deserted sidewalk near the door, his face an ashy gray. "Little" Wilbur, in Hugh's mind, though a man as tall as himself. No greetings. "Come on," Hugh said, unlocking the door, and led him through the reception room to his spacious office in back. All strange, somehow, with Wilbur there, Wilbur and now, like accompaniment, the muted tones of a church bell ringing in the distance. Sunday, Hugh remembered. Instead of behind his desk as habit inclined him, he sat down in one of the chairs where his clients always sat. "You too," he said, and Wilbur took the chair that faced his own, saying, "Is it true, what I heard? That she did it to herself?"

That ashen face. Even his eyes, once gander-blue, were not as Hugh remembered them . . . dull now, reddened with his grief. "Yes," he softly said and then, as if one Yes was not enough, repeated it. "With sleeping tablets. A dozen or so, we think. Sometime in the night. I didn't find her till almost noon, when she didn't come down. She was still alive then, but just barely."

Wilbur opened his mouth but did not speak. For an interval he rested his face in his hands. "You were the one that found her, then. Where was her mother?"

"She wasn't at home. Out somewhere." Just out, he thought, recalling his glimpse of her leaving when he came down.

The silence now stretched out for a while. Suddenly, his ashen face exposed again, "Why?" he said with passion.

Tell him? How much? "She was unhappy. I'm sure of that much."

Wilbur's gaze was fastened on him. "What else, that you're not sure of?"

Hugh groped for an answer.

Wilbur said, "I knew she was unhappy, too. And I knew it was about her mother. I saw that when she came to see me. She wouldn't let it come clear out, but I could tell . . . It was like her mother kept her under a spell, all her life . . . something the poor child couldn't break out of, no matter what. That woman . . ." He paused as if to restrain the passion reflected in his eyes.

"It's all right," Hugh said. "Go on."

"All those years and I never knew her. But I know her now, better than ever. You know the McDougal woman?"

"I know about her."

"She moved away right after that. The disgrace and all. I found out where she moved to and went to see her. Finally, day before yesterday. It was Nora that sent her to the police for the warrant. She told her things, lies. That she had seen the priest, with her own eyes, fondling that little girl. Even kissing her. And other such lies. She . . ."

"Did she, the McDougal woman, think they were lies?"

"No. She's still deceived . . . halfway, anyhow. But I'm not. I got the details out of her. And you know what's worst of all?" He paused for a second as if he thought that Hugh might have the answer.

Hugh shook his head.

"She brought Jean in, in person, to testify to her lies."

There was silence, or almost silence, for that bell was ringing again. Finally, and weakly, Hugh said, "But you don't know they were lies."

"Sure I know. Think about it. That she saw it happening. And things Jean knew, had overheard. The only thing really hard to figure is why she hated the priest that much. I remember her feelings about religion. But this . . . it's diabolical, or something."

The bell had stopped. Hugh sat looking at his hands, one objection and then another asserting itself and fading from his mind.

"So I'm wondering," Wilbur quietly said. "About Jean."

Hugh looked up. "No. She did it. She got the pills from our bathroom."

The reddened eyes regarded him. "Driven, then."

Driven? Slowly Hugh got up from his chair. "You have to be wrong."

Wilbur shook his head. Then, "One more thing. What about a funeral? Or will there be one?"

"No. She's being cremated."

"And that's all?"

"Yes."

"I guessed as much. Cremated. The right word, here." Then, getting onto his feet he said, "I want her ashes."

"All right," Hugh said.

He sat in his car for a long time before he drove home. Blessedly she was not there and he did not allow himself even to wonder where she had gone. Maybe she would not come back. But he knew she would and after an hour he heard her car in the drive.

It was a difficult and bewildering day, one he would remember all his life. For most of it, by stratagems and unwitting help from those who came to visit, he was able to stay clear of her presence. But there were intervals. The first one followed her arrival after his meeting with Wilbur. She stopped in the door of the den where he was seated, a magazine idly in his hands.

"What did he want?" she said.

He looked up at her rigid face, a face not beautiful now, then looked away. "To hear about Jean."

"What about her?"

"How she died."

She waited. "No mention of me, I suppose?"

"Just in passing." Her hair was awry, strangely wild.

"Liar. Both of you, liars." She turned and went to the stairs and up.

Another event took place in the night, one like, though with embellishments, that one in the afternoon. But now he was not in their bedroom when it happened. In the den in the shaded light of a lamp, sleepless and brooding on the sofa, he noticed first a scent as of flowers gathering around him. She was there, in the sheerest of her gowns, with hair now coiffed and lips defined in the pallor of her face. Leaning down, making place beside him, she softly said, "Hugh. I want you back." Her hand lay on his chest. "The way we were before." When he did not answer she said, "It's just the shock, what I'm going through. I'm the same." Then, "Come up to bed. Please."

For a still moment he was moved by a flickering of desire. It passed and in the enduring stillness he could only think to say, "Not now," and later add, "I'm sorry."

The silence gathered. He felt her stir and draw away, had a glimpse of her face above him. Her slippered feet made only a whisper of sound when she left the room.

Along in the night he heard her moving about, twice descending the stairs, then up again. And several times, in a dream or not, he thought he heard voices whispering and, once, a cry. When he woke up, later in the morning than was his custom, he found that she was gone.

21

IT WAS A COUPLE OF DAYS before Hugh was able to get the whole story straight. The first part, or most of it, came from Wilbur's secretary, Miss Miller. When she came to work that Monday morning around nine o'clock she noticed an elegantly dressed woman she did not know. The woman was seated on a bench just inside the entrance to the building where the mailboxes were. This was odd, and her apparent nervousness, her shifting gaze and tensely folded hands, made it more so. Miss Miller went on up to the office and set about getting some papers in order.

Half an hour or so later the office door opened and that same woman entered. She stood there for a moment without speaking, long enough for Miss Miller to notice a difference in her appearance. It was her hair, as though she had been running her fingers through it, leaving it in disarray. After that moment the woman asked, as she must have known already, whether Mr. Helton was in. When the answer was No, she asked when he was likely to get there. He was in court, Miss Miller told her, and it probably would be a while. Somehow this information seemed to reassure the woman. Without a word she stepped across the room and sat down in one of the chairs to wait.

What for? Besides this question, the woman's mere presence, with her busy fingers and the silent movement of her lips, was unnerving to Miss Miller. She tried to do her work with the papers but her eyes kept glancing back at the woman in the chair. Or, after the first few minutes, sometimes in the chair. She kept getting up and standing at the window to view the street below. What was her name, her purpose here? More and more Miss Miller began to feel that she was in the presence of someone dangerous, maybe insane. After what must have been nearly an hour she recalled, gratefully, that it was time to go down and get the mail.

When she got back with several letters and a large manilla envelope in her hand, the woman was standing up, waiting for her. Miss Miller went around to her chair and, sitting down, put the mail on the desk top. Then came the woman's hand, reaching for it. Miss Miller was a gutsy person and she snatched it back out of the hand's reach. Angrily she said, "These are for Mr. Helton."

"That one," the woman said, her finger pointing at a letter shakily addressed. "I made a mistake, misaddressed it. Let me have it, please."

Miss Miller's hackles were up. "I will not. Not without Mr. Helton's approval."

"Wait," the woman said and stepped to the chair where her purse lay. She came back with a check and held it out for Miss Miller to read. Astonishingly, it was for five thousand dollars. "This and you don't tell him. Or any one. Ever."

Miss Miller could not help but hesitate for a few seconds, but only a few. Moving her hand with the letter still farther away she said, "You'll have to wait for Mr. Helton."

This was the moment that fastened itself most vividly in her memory. It was of the woman's eyes upon her, dark eyes but with an illumination like the devil's own. Of what followed, her recollections were a little blurred. There was a struggle, in which the woman had her by the arm in a grip more powerful than Miss Miller could have imagined possible, tearing with her other hand at the letter that Miss Miller now held tight in her own. Then the stab of pain that made Miss Miller cry out. It was the letter opener, buried deep in her arm. The woman had drawn back, with the crushed letter in her hand.

But a blessed thing happened. The woman had already taken a step toward the door when it suddenly opened. A man stood there, blocking her way. It was Mr. Helton, standing there with his mouth open.

Miss Miller's voice, almost a scream: "She's got your letter! She took it from me!" On her feet now, she was holding out her bloody arm for view.

There was a pause in which Wilbur merely stared at his former wife, at the letter crushed in her hand. Another man appeared behind him.

"It's my letter," she said, blazing at Wilbur. "I misaddressed it."

"Let me have it," Wilbur said, stepping forward.

She stepped back, put it behind her, was trying to tear it apart by the time he reached her.

The new man on the scene described her resistence. He said she fought like an animal, tooth and claw, bloodying Wilbur's face. He did not blame Wilbur for finally hitting her, very hard, knocking her to the floor. He got the letter. He had it open, was reading it by the time she got to her feet. She moved, shakily at first, bumped against the man standing near the door, and fled.

It was not until next day that Hugh read the letter. There was not much of it, in pencil, awkwardly written. "I did it for Mama. What she told me to say. About the priest. She made me think it was true. It was wicked. I am so sorry. I love you." The letter was unsigned.

By this time Hugh had heard where Nora went directly after leaving Wilbur's office. Whether in confusion or in fear of going home she had gone to what Hugh had learned was her private spot, the little restaurant down on Water Street. The proprietor, Mr. Krantz, had described what it was like to see her come in as she did, with bruised bloody lips, and hair and clothes awry. He thought at first that she might be about to do something wild and destructive in his restaurant, that she had gone mad. But she took her regular booth and sat like a stone, not even acknowledging his tardy offer to serve her. She ignored the coffee he brought, ignored everything, just sat staring at the big plate glass window that faced the street. At last she got up suddenly and left without paying.

Ella Hobbs, the black cleaning woman, was at the house that day at noon, having just arrived when Nora's car stopped in front of the garage. Ella saw her get out and stand looking about her before she turned and approached the back door. The look of her frightened the old woman. She tried to speak and failed, and Nora, as if blind to her presence, passed her by and went upstairs. She stayed for a little while. Ella, not dangerously close to the stairway, stood in nervous attention to the sounds of Nora's bustling about up there. But, by her account, she had heard more than these bustling sounds. She swore that she had heard voices, the second one a man's voice.

She had quickly fled to the kitchen door when Nora started down. But from there she could still see the foot of the steps and Nora who had come to a halt with a suitcase in her hand. (It contained, as was later discovered, her finest garments and all her valuable jewelry.) Her manner was different now, deliberate. She put the suitcase down. She went into the den, out of sight, and for several minutes there was silence. In something of a hurry now she reappeared and picked up the suitcase. Once more, on her way out through the kitchen, she gave no sign of noticing Ella. But there was something else. In passing she had come close enough for Ella to get a whiff of what was plainly not the perfume that Nora habitually wore. "It were a kind of a stink, like," Ella said. "Somethin' ugly. It were like it got stuck in my nose and wouldn't get out that whole day long."

It was a minute or two later that Ella, standing in the back door now, became conscious of two things at almost the same time. One of these, she said, though with some appearance of uncertainty, was that as the car drove away Nora was not at the wheel but on the side toward Ella, in the passenger seat.

But this moment of perplexity was immediately swallowed up by a more startling one. She smelled smoke. She turned around. Indeed there was smoke. She hurried and from the hall could see that the beautiful flowered drapes in the den were ablaze. She approached and then drew back and rushed to the telephone. The firemen arrived in time to save the greater part of the house.

The final event was reported to Hugh that night by the police. There had been a wreck, a fatal one. Her car had run off the highway, through a guardrail and down a steep embankment. It had turned over several times and then had burst into flame. Even before the fire was finally put out, they could see her charred body inside the car.

One of the two strange things involved was how it happened. There had been a car following behind her, on a straight stretch of highway. The driver gave the description. The two cars were moving at the same fair rate of speed and he so far had not seen any sign of erratic driving on the part of the driver ahead. But suddenly, for no apparent reason, that car swerved, sharply, and crashed through the guardrail and on. The other strange thing was that the driver behind declared with near certainty that he had seen, had kept seeing, two people in that car. If so, there was no evidence of the whereabouts of the second occupant.

ತಿ ತಿ ತಿ

Five days later, three days after the hurried and barely decent interment of Nora, there was another burial. This one too was informal, but only outwardly. It took place in the small maple-shaded graveyard beside the burned-out church. Hugh, arriving just before sunset, stepping out of his car, saw among the gravestones over beyond the ruins his brother standing, very still, close beside a tree trunk. "Still" was the word: the word for his brother's figure, for the absence of the faintest breeze to trouble the pendant foliage, for even the last late slant of light as if the sun had paused in its procession. One thing more caught his attention. It was there as before, in the surviving section of wall at the back corner, in the pointed arch of the window. Still there in a fragment of colored glass, the head and shoulders of Christ ascending above the aperture. Hugh took the shovel out of his trunk.

The little urn of ashes stood on the ground next to their mother's stone. Hugh lifted his eyes and found his brother's gaze upon him, as though with some kind of a question. Despite this new gauntness of Wilbur's face, the sunken eyes encircled with darkness, Hugh was suddenly struck with the thought that the face was like a rough copy of his own. Then Wilbur spoke. "Let's get on with it."

"All right," Hugh said, lifting the shovel. "Is this where you want it . . . just where it is?"

"Yes." Wilbur said. "But let me do it."

"Sure," Hugh said, handing over the shovel.

Wilbur's thrusts with the shovel were slow, though the ground itself was easy, dark rich ground turned up with little effort. Finally, "Deep enough?" he said.

"I think so."

"Then I'll do it." He laid the shovel aside, but when he reached for the urn Hugh was there to hand it to him. He put it in, settling it some two feet deep, and afterward remained through a long silent minute there on his knees. Then he stood up. "There ought to be some words said."

"I guess so." Hugh cast about among his rusty memories, but it was Wilbur who, a little shamefaced even now, came up with something: the Paternoster, which he recited just above a whisper. He took up the shovel and covered the urn and afterward with his hands patted smooth the little mound of dirt. "We'll have the stone in a few days," he said.

When, minutes later, a breath of air came and stirred the foliage, Hugh broke their silence. "Father Riley's dead, you know. Finally. Just a couple of days ago."

"Yes, I heard."

"They'll send another one."

Wilbur faintly nodded.

"I guess you knew they've decided to build the church back. I saw a list of a lot of people who've promised contributions. You'll be surprised. Even that lout Blankenship, a big one. Hard to imagine."

Wilbur nodded again. His gaze now was on the stone, the one head-tall, with all the family names. He said, "I'm glad we put her here."

"Sure," Hugh said and fell quiet for a little space. Then, "You like to think that everybody's feeling a little penitent, for a change. But I guess they'll recover pretty soon."

"I guess so," Wilbur said. "But maybe not, you can't tell. Things happen . . . for the good sometimes. Maybe this is one of the times."

"I hope so. I'd hate to think the poor man's death didn't accomplish anything at all." He paused. "One thing, though, at least. It did give us a new start."

Wilbur was silent for a moment. With a glance at Hugh, he said, "More than that, maybe . . . when you think about it. A lot more."

Hugh did not understand at first. It was Wilbur's glance, slow to reveal its meaning, that now brought "her" to his mind's eye. He thrust her away, rid of her . . . he and everyone. "I see what you mean. I guess you can think of it that way."

ABOUT THE AUTHOR

Madison Jones is the author of several novels, including *The Innocent, A Cry of Absence, A Buried Land, An Exile, Last Things, To the Winds,* and *Nashville 1864: The Dying of the Light.* He has received fellowships from the Rockefeller Foundation, *The Sewanee Review,* and the Guggenheim Foundation. His works have been published in *Washington Post Book World, The New York Times Book Review, The Southern Review,* and *The Sewanee Review.* His awards include the T. S. Eliot Award from the Ingersoll Foundation; The Harper Lee Award; The Michael Shaara Award from The United States Civil War Center and a Lytle Short Story Prize from *The Sewanee Review.* He lives in Auburn, Alabama.

Deep South Books

THE UNIVERSITY OF ALABAMA PRESS

Vicki Covington
Gathering Home

Vicki Covington
The Last Hotel for Women

Nanci Kincaid
Crossing Blood

Paul Hemphill
Leaving Birmingham: Notes of a Native Son

Roy Hoffman
Almost Family

Helen Norris
One Day in the Life of a Born Again Loser

Patricia Foster
All the Lost Girls: Confessions of a Southern Daughter

Sam Hodges
B-4

Howell Raines
Whiskey Man

Judith Hillman Paterson
Sweet Mystery: A Book of Remembering

Mary Ward Brown
Tongues of Flame

Jay Lamar and Jeanie Thompson, eds.
The Remembered Gate: Memoirs by Alabama Writers

Mary Ward Brown
It Wasn't All Dancing and Other Stories

Eugene Walter
The Untidy Pilgrim

Julia Oliver
Goodbye to the Buttermilk Sky

Lee May
In My Father's Garden

Don Keith
The Forever Season

Kelly Cherry
My Life and Dr. Joyce Brothers: A Novel in Stories

Madison Jones
Herod's Wife